A ROGER HARPER NOVEL

THE MAN WHO COULD NOT CHEAT TIME

JAMES G RILEY
BERNADINE RILEY

THE MAN WHO COULD NOT CHEAT TIME

A ROGER HARPER NOVEL

JAMES G RILEY

BERNADINE RILEY

ABOUT THE AUTHORS

James and Bernadine live in Florida with their dog, Barkley. They have nine wonderful grandchildren; six girls and three boys.

James taught math and economics whilst living in England. In California and Arizona, he worked as a banker, stockbroker, and insurance agent.

As well as being a homemaker, Bernadine, at one time, owned a book and gift store. She assisted in the research and editing of the first Roger Harper novel *The Man Who Would Cheat At Cards*. This is the third book they have authored together, the others being *The Man Who Would Stop A Clock and The Boy Who Wasn't There.*

For more information visit: jamesgriley.com

Email: jamesandbernadine@jamesgriley.com

a   amazon.com/author.jamesgriley

f   facebook.com/jamesgriley.author

o   instagram.com/jamesgriley.author

g   goodreads.com/jamesgriley

p   pinterest.com/jamesgrileyauthor

ALSO BY JAMES G RILEY

OTHER ROGER HARPER NOVELS

(Book 1) The Man Who Would Cheat At Cards

ISBN: 978-1-944108-04-5

SAMPLE REVIEW

★ ★ ★ ★ ★

Wonderfully written and cleverly intense.

A delightfully well-written thriller with incredible detail to description. I was thoroughly impressed from start to finish. The poker scene was well crafted and intense. A must-read for anyone looking for action and thrills

(Book 2) The Man Who Would Stop A Clock

Co-written with Bernadine Riley

SAMPLE REVIEW

★ ★ ★ ★

An intriguing plot

I wondered before I started just how the title of the book would be relevant to what is at once a thriller, a mystery, and a who-done-it. Certainly, the way it was done is very clever. This is a great story and very well told.

(Book 4) The Boy Who Wasn't There

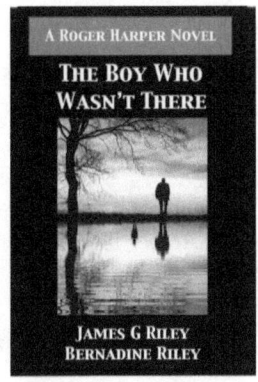

★★★★★

Entertaining and Educational

James and Bernadine Riley have done it again. No more emerging writers: they have emerged. A great blend of narrative and dialogue awaits you. Characters and location development transport you throughout the story. Excellent plot development with good entry and exit hooks makes it easy to turn the page for the next reveal. The intermingling of fantasy and reality engages the readers' imagination while the story moves from subplot to subplot. If you want to be casually educated and entertained while you read, this book and the rest of the Harper series are for you.

A Sᴘᴇᴄɪᴀʟ Aɢᴇɴᴛ Aʟʟᴇɴ Rɪᴄʜᴀʀᴅsᴏɴ Mʏsᴛᴇʀʏ

Lab Rats

★★★★★

Warning this may test your imagination

Talk about imagination. Jim tested mine with Lab Rats. The plotline is unique, and his characters come to life. His description of the caves is outstanding - I thought I was there and somewhat claustrophobic :) Great read.

Merry Dance

JAMES G RILEY

MERRY DANCE

A COLLECTION OF
SHORT STORIES &
POEMS

★★★★★

Mystery and fantasy for all ages

Every story was a surprise. Jim's imagination is off the charts. You will enjoy each of these stories for their uniqueness. Delightful.

★★★★

Entertaining short reads

This charming collection of fanciful stories and poems is the perfect antidote to a long wait in a doctor's office. It will likely amuse and pique the curiosity of readers trapped on a boring train or plane ride. The author doesn't always solve the paranormal problems he presents, but pondering them will make for an entertaining short read.

A QUEST FOR KING ARTHUR SERIES

Conundrum (A Quest For King Arthur § Book One)

CONUNDRUM
A QUEST FOR KING
ARTHUR
BOOK ONE

JAMES G RILEY

★★

The premise was good

I believe that the author shows promise. The story threads come together in the last quarter of the book.

Amulet (A Quest For King Arthur §
Book Two)

★★★★★

I highly recommend it

James G Riley opens his second novel in a series with a well-written summation of his first book for those not familiar with Part One. His novel is clever by every measure. It's a retelling of a classic tale, with a twist involving time travel and bi-located settings in the years 2016 and 546. We get the pleasure of reacquainting ourselves with the classic characters in King Arthur's world, as well as being introduced to their modern-day counterparts thrust into the past. The details of the adventures are vivid. Riley thoroughly researched his material. His writing is transportive, educational, and entertaining throughout. *Amulet* is worth the read for anyone loving the concept of time travel and the challenge to solve riddles to advance the storyline.

DISCLAIMERS

This is a work of fiction. Names, characters, businesses, places, events, and incidents are either the products of the author's imagination or used in a fictitious manner. Any resemblance to actual persons, living or dead, or actual events is purely coincidental.

Trademarks are property of their respective owners. The author is not associated with any product or vendor mentioned in this book.

ACKNOWLEDGMENTS

I would like to express my sincere thanks to Bernadine, who collaborated in the writing, assisted with the editing, proofreading, and design of this book.
Thank you.

Authors' portrait photograph by Amanda Rose Day

DEDICATION

To Our Grandchildren
Reading is to the mind what exercise is to the body.

PROLOGUE

PALACIO PRESIDENCIA, LA HABANA, APRIL 1957

"*INFORME* [REPORT]," FULGENCIO BATISTA DEMANDED OF POLICE *Captán* Esteban Ventura, who stood in front of his desk.

"*Señor Presidente*, we raided an apartment building in Humboldt Street, as you instructed, and found six members of the *Directorio Revolucionario* hiding there. A shootout ensued in which Fructuoso Rodríguez, one of the *DR* founders, was killed, together with three others."

"The other two?" Batista asked.

"They have escaped, but we know their names; Faure Chaumon and Raúl Díaz Argüelle. My men are searching for them as we speak, *General*."

"Very good, *Captán*. Keep me updated on any new developments."

"*Sí, señor Presidente*."

Ventura remained at attention in front of Batista.

"You are dismissed, *Captán*. Tell my secretary to come in as you leave."

The policeman did not move.

"Are you deaf, *Captán*? *Despedido!*"

Ventura opened his mouth and then closed it.

"If you have something else to say, man, spit it out."

"*Señor Presidente*, there has been an incident at *del Hospital de Dementes de Santamaria*. Twenty-six patients have died from neglect and malnutrition."

"I am sure the *Ministerio de Salibridad* [Ministry of Health] will deal with it. Probably close it down. That will be a good thing too. Having a lunatic asylum on the outskirts of the city is bad for tourism. Why are you wasting my time telling me this?"

"People are clamoring for the arrest of the doctors at the hospital."

"Then arrest them. You don't need me to tell you how to do your job. Now go, *Captán*, before I lose my temper."

"But *General*; if I am not mistaken, I believe el Director of the hospital, *señor* Carlos Fuentes, is a close friend of yours."

"Quite so, *Captán*, quite so. Leave the matter with me. Busy yourself finding those two participants in the March 13th Palace attack."

Captán Ventura saluted and left. Batista picked up the telephone.

"Carlos, listen to me. You should leave the country as quickly as possible. Are your research papers somewhere safe? We do not want the formula falling into the wrong hands."

"Do you know, Fulgencio, you worry too much? I have my bags packed already. Just a couple of things to take care of, and I shall be on my way. *Adiós, viejo amigo.*"

THE SOUND OF FIST STRIKING JAW MAY NOT HAVE REVERBERATED around the interrogation room, but the recipient felt the blow rattle the inside of his skull. "Ouch."

"Ouch? Ouch is all you can say, Harper?" The speaker, the third man in the brightly lit room with its easy-to-clean wall tiles, moved to stand inches away, so close the smell of tobacco was discernible upon his breath. "Do you understand, we're not pussyfooting around, my friend? Give it up, Harper, or Knuckles, here, will loosen one or two of your front teeth. Do you like the nickname Knuckles? I thought it up myself. Rather good, don't you think?"

"You're a double douchebag, do you know that, Midnight?" Harper was addressing his onetime friend, Kurt Mitchell. Eleven years ago, they had conspired together to cheat at cards, winning the pot in a ten million dollar poker tournament by exploiting Harper's ability to read the other players' minds. And then Mitchell had betrayed him in an attempt to keep the prize money all to himself. Nevertheless, Mitchell had paid the price of duplicity, or so Harper thought, by being thrown off a bridge into the icy waters below. Somehow the traitor had survived. Now, standing there gloating, he had the upper hand.

"I told the FBI, the Camp Commandant, and I'm telling you; I refuse to use my mind-reading ability to interrogate the prisoners locked up in this wretched place. Beating the shit out of me isn't going to change my mind."

Mitchell laughed. "Roger, Roger, Roger." Harper hated anyone but his wife, Julia, from addressing him by his first name. "We're not here to instill in you a sense of patriotism. What I require from you is the number of the Swiss bank account where you keep my money."

"Your money? How do you figure it's your money."

"Because you stole my share of the poker winnings. I merely want to collect my dues," Mitchell replied. "With interest, of course."

"In your dreams, Midnight. In your dreams."

Mitchell nodded to Knuckles, a brute of a man over six feet tall, weighing over three hundred pounds.

"Fugh," Harper screamed. "Yuv boke muh jaw."

In response, Mitchell grinned. "Don't insult my man. He's a professional. He hasn't broken your jaw, Roger. Just dislocated it a little; that's all. Do the honors, Knuckles. We can't have our friend speaking funny; now can we?"

There was a cracking sound, followed by more screaming as Knuckles popped Harper lower mandrel back into place.

"Don't be such a baby," Mitchell counseled. "Do everyone a favor and tell me what I need to know before Knuckles becomes impatient for his cut."

"What's he going to do next; waterboard me?"

"Roger, Roger. I wouldn't dream of such a thing. However, Knuckles does have a chemist friend who is rather good at administering very unpleasant injections. It will take a day or two to set up. After that, you won't be able to resist. You'll be singing like a canary." Mitchell looked at his wristwatch. "Still, I can't stand around chatting with you all day. It's time for lunch. First, however, we'll get you back to your cozy little cell. Remind me, before I leave, to tell the chef to liquidize your meals for a while," he added with a chuckle.

THE MORNING FOLLOWING HARPER'S ENCOUNTER WITH MIDNIGHT and Knuckles, he lay on his cot, inside what was known as Camp Five Echo. Along with two dozen other prisoners, he was held in the disciplinary block for *noncompliant* prisoners. Their cells were too small to be regarded as humane, with inadequate squat toilets set into the floor, excessively bright lighting, and air that was a foul mix of sweat and human excrement.

One of the detainees, presumably a self-elected *muezzin*, called the inmates to prayer.

Meaning no disrespect, Harper tuned out the sound as his thoughts turned to his wife Julia, and his son Oliver, who he had abruptly left on the steps of St. Paul's Cathedral at the time of his arrest. He wondered if they had made it to the home of Julia's Aunt Cordelia in Savannah, Georgia. If so, what were the two of them doing now? *The two of them?* Harper was forgetting; Julia was pregnant at the time of his departure. He wondered when was the baby due. However, the date eluded him.

Separated from the cell itself by rows of steel bars, Harper stared at the roof space. A shiver went down his back as he recalled Mitchell's treat of a chemist who was rather good at administering painful injections. *What were that prick's exact words? "It will take a day or two to set up." I've got to get out of this place before then*, he told himself, as a passing guard took a discreet drag on a cigarette. *Things have become lapse around here*, he observed. *That's a weak link I can exploit. Right?*

In his head, Harper mulled through the problem, searching for answers.

Escape
    How?
Through the roof?
    Not easy with the steel bars, although there is a maintenance hatch below the light fitting.
Through the cell door?
    Not unless a guard obligingly unlocks it for me.
What would make a guard let me out?
    An emergency.
What type of emergency?
    A fire.
A fire, where?
    In the roof space?
How to gain access?
    Not easy with the steel bars.

Damn it. I'm back where I started.

"Damn it, damn it, damn it," Harper repeated, this time cursing out loud, which drew the attention of the inmate whose cell was on the other side of the passageway.

As if he were a psychiatrist addressing a patient, the man wearing the same orange jumpsuit inquired, "Is there something you want to talk about, my friend?"

It was the first time Harper had taken any notice of this fellow detainee. Curly-haired, cut in a shaggy bob, with a beard trimmed shorter than the majority of inmates, he did not stand out from the crowd. Not until he spoke, that is. His English was impeccable, delivered with an almost musical flow that seems to be common to speakers of Romance languages.

"You speak English?" Harper counted, sounding surprised.

"Of course. They taught me when I was at school in Salvador. Founded by the Portuguese in 1549 as the first capital of Brazil, Salvador is one of the oldest colonial cities in the Americas. Did you know that?" Harper shook his head, wondering why a Brazilian was imprisoned at Guantanamo. "By the way, my name is Federico Ramírez."

"Pleased to meet you, Federico. My name is Harper."

"Harper, hum. That is an interesting name. Originally that given to a player of the harp. The *harper* was one of the most important figures of a medieval baronial hall, especially in Scotland and northern England. Often the office of *harper* was hereditary. But I expect you knew that already."

"No, I didn't," the American admitted. "Harper is my family name. I prefer not to use my first name." There was a pause as he further reflected on Federico's first remarks. Then he continued, "Let me get this straight. You went to school in Brazil, and now you are in here, interned as a terrorist?"

"That's how they mistakenly classify me. Nobody would listen when I told them I was a war correspondent. My own fault. I never bothered to get the proper credentials before I became embedded with the freedom fighters. The fact I was holding a rifle did not help my case when I was captured. But that was only to make myself blend in and not look like a reporter."

"Terrorists are terrorists in my book; not freedom fighters," Harper responded, contemptuously. "To me, it sounds as if you drank too much Kool-Aid, buddy. And reporters don't usually carry guns."

"Don't be so judgmental," Federico countered. "Nelson Mandela was labeled a terrorist once. Later he became President of South Africa."

Choosing not to enter into a debate about international politics, Harper replied, "If you say so, Federico," before turning on his cot to face the wall.

There was a lull in the conversation, broken when the Brazilian asked, "Harper, you are American; am I right?"

"That should be self-evident. I'm a freedom fighter, like yourself, can't you tell?" Harper responded, facetiously. "Now leave me alone. I'm thinking."

Federico persisted. "Americans who break the law are locked up in American jails, I believe. So, why are you here, in the same cellblock as me?"

Deciding the only way to be left alone was to answer the question, he rolled over and replied, "It's a long story, Federico."

The other inmate laughed. "And you are short of time, I suppose? Do you have an appointment to be elsewhere? Tell me, please."

"Oh, very well." Harper sat up, scratched the stubble on his chin, deciding he would get little peace by ignoring the request. "If you must know, I was brought here because the Authorities had the mistaken belief that I would help them with the interrogation of prisoners. But I refused. Then they thought spending some time in this home away from home would change my mind. It hasn't."

"Yesterday, they beat you badly. Am I right? I see your black eyes and bruised jaw."

"I refused to divulge some information. In a day or two, the interrogator will likely administer drugs to make me talk. Consequently, I need to get out of this place as soon as possible."

"You have a plan to break out?"

"You know, I just might," Harper replied, as the whiff of the guard's tobacco smoke assaulted his nostrils. "But I'll need your help if I'm to escape."

"Escape," Federico repeated, with emphasis. "Certainly, I will, but only if you agree to take me with you. I know the island well and have friends here too."

"Very well," Harper agreed. "We have a deal."

3

THE JEEP CAPTAIN VICKERS WAS DRIVING CAME TO A SLITHERING halt outside Cell Bock C, sending clouds of dust into the air. He was responding to an incident. Stomping through the entryway, his disposition did not improve when he discovered the call-out was the result of half a dozen blown light bulbs.

"How did this happen?" he demanded, in a foul-tempered manner, having been forced to leave the air-conditioning enjoyed in the Officers' Mess.

"I don't know, sir. I was at the other end of the block at the time," the guard on duty replied.

"I don't suppose anyone thought to send for an electrician?"

"I thought it best you were informed first, Captain. I'll call straight away."

"Be sure you do. Tell Sergeant Johnson to have these six cells emptied as quickly possible. Move the inmates to Block Bravo until the lights are back on. Anything else I need to know?"

"No, sir."

"Very well. See to it."

Without further ado, Vickers swaggered out of the door. As he headed back to the Officers' Mess, he cursed at the fact that his lunch had been disrupted.

Harper lurked at the back of his cell, watching as the affected inmates were being moved. Federico winked in his direction when it became the Brazilian's turn. Twenty minutes earlier, Harper had used his telekinetic power to compress the light bulbs until they imploded. Six in all, which was the maximum in the American's line of sight as he had pressed himself against the cell bars and squinted along the corridor.

Now all he had to do was wait

Captain Vickers was called away from his table to the telephone. Sergeant Johnson informed him the prisoners had been relocated, and the electrician was on site.

"That's good news. Any idea of the cause, Sergeant?"

"Not really, sir. The electrician says it's not a faulty circuit breaker. The box was replaced less than a year ago."

"What then?" Vickers asked, tapping his chest, trying to relieve his indigestion.

"He says it could be that when one bulb blew, it took out the next. However, to have half a dozen go at the same time is most unusual."

"But, he can fix them?"

"Of course, sir."

"When do you expect to have the prisoners back in their cells?"

"That depends, Captain. Because of the security bolts on the access hatches, he has had to return to the maintenance storeroom to pick up a special tool. Could be an hour or more before he is back."

"An hour, or more. Why so long?"

"He didn't say, sir. I'll let you know when everything is back to normal. Enjoy your lunch, Captain."

Vickers slammed down the phone, burped loudly, and headed for the bar. He ordered a double scotch and sat moodily gazing out of the Mess window.

Two drinks later, the Captain had mellowed somewhat, grateful he did not have to endure the sweatbox of Five Echo.

Harper, on the other hand, lacking an open bar, enjoyed no such creature comforts. However, *everything is relative*, he decided, as he watched the electrician climb up a ladder and wrestle with the security bolts in Federico's cell before he could gain access to the light fitting and change the bulb. Having repeated the task for the sixth time, the man's coverall was drenched in sweat.

As he lounged on his cot, the American reflected on events of the previous four weeks.

He had been instrumental in the recovery of paintings stolen from London's art galleries. An action, in the words of Britain's Prime Minister, which *"will earn you a mention in dispatches."* A hollow promise. Contrary to Harper's expectation of being awarded nothing less than the Order of the British Empire, he received not a thing. The only *OBE* foisted in his direction was an *Out-of-the-Blue Extradition*, ostensibly to the States, but in reality to the Naval Base at Guantanamo, Cuba.

Accompanied by two FBI Agents named Jones and Delaney, he initially believed he was to face charges of allegedly killing CEO Geoffrey Phelps and private investigator Marcus Willoughby. In truth, Phelps had shot Willoughby, who later died of his wounds, and then turned the gun on himself. The fact the dead PI had been entombed in the wall of his own office did nothing to help Harper's defense.

Notwithstanding, Roger Harper was not destined to face a judge in an American courtroom. Instead, he was expected to help with the interrogation of prisoners held at the detention camp, using his ability to read people's minds. As an inducement, if Harper were successful in gaining useful intel, the charges against him would be dropped.

In the beginning, they treated me with sweetness and light, he recalled. Assigned a *separate billet in the Officers' Quarters, and allowed to roam freely about the base, should I choose. However, once it became clear I was not going to cooperate, the base commander decided a little coercion was in order.*

Slumming it with the enlisted men had been the first step. An uncomfortable bed with a lumpy mattress was the least of his problems. Treated like a rookie, constant hazing by the other occupants of the dormitory had made Harper's life a living hell.

Then the CO had resorted to playing good cop, trying to appeal to Harper's sense of duty. That did not work, so he was unceremoniously escorted to the Detention Center and became a detainee, not a member of the staff.

Harper's thoughts drifted back to Kirt Mitchell's part in all this. Mitchell had helped during the arrest in London and the extradition, by thwarting any attempt Harper might make to trick his way to freedom. Mitchell also was in residence at the Naval Station and, for a time, continued to monitor Harper, stopping him from interfering with personnel in a way that might have enabled an escape. But Mitchell got bored and was preparing to leave. As a parting present, he told the Authorities that a foil-lined hat was an effective way to keep Harper out of their heads. Now the cellblock guards wore special helmets, thwarting any attempt at implanting the idea he was a prime candidate for release.

The American let out a deep sigh. What had happened was in the past. Now it was time to look to the future. *So far, the escape plan is on track*, Harper told himself. The electrician, who had not been wearing a foil-lined helmet, had absentmindedly left the special security-bolt remover on Federico's cot, an action predicated by Harper's subliminal thought-implant. The American smiled with satisfaction. *As soon as Federico and the other prisoners return to their cells, I can embark on the next phase. All being well, tomorrow I'll be out of this place and a free man.*

4

WITH A START, HARPER WOKE FROM HIS UNSCHEDULED CATNAP. HE had been dreaming of scented jasmine that filled a garden where children were playing on the lawn. His wife had just come out of the house carrying a tray of freshly made lemonade. However, the all-intrusive stench attacking his nostrils brought the American back to reality.

The guard had returned. Standing in front of the cell opposite, he was talking to the occupant. The conversation was friendly enough. Following Harper's plan, Federico politely asked for a smoke.

"And why should I do that?" the Brazilian was asked.

"I have seen the look of disgust on your face when you see how some of us prisoners are being mistreated. I think you did not volunteer to be assigned to this camp, and you would rather be somewhere else. Deep down, you are a good person. Please, I am begging you for a smoke."

Federico had clearly struck a chord, for the guard obliged. Taking the cigarette, the inmate asked for a light. The guard fumbled for his lighter.

Harper immediately switched to telepathic mode. He tuned into the mind of the belligerent inmate further along the block, who had caused a ruckus the day before.

Throw your bed against the wall. See if you can draw in another sucker so he may enjoy a dollop of your saliva.

Nothing happened. Harper knew the man spoke English. *What is stopping him*, he wondered?

Who are you? The words floated out of the other man's mind.

I am a messenger. They treat you like a pig. Why are you waiting?

Harper looked nervously across the aisle. The guard was holding out his lighter and was about to flick a light for Federico's cigarette.

برو به جهنم

The inmate's response resonated inside Harper's head. Although he understood not a word, from the aggressive tone, he imagined it was not an everyday *hello* or *how are you?*

The American was running out of time. If he had not fallen asleep, he could have prepped the other inmate sooner.

It's only right they receive the same treatment. Harper made one final desperate attempt to get the prisoner to respond. *Go on, do it!*

Seconds passed. Federico looked nervously in Harper's direction, hanging back as long as he could.

"Do want a smoke or not?" the guard asked.

Federico answered that he did.

The sound of a bed frame striking blockwork and then clattered to the floor, echoed down the corridor. Manic laughter followed.

"What the fuck! Here take this. I'll be back in a sec." The guard sprinted towards the commotion, leaving Federico clutching the precious lighter.

Shouting was heard in the distance.

"Enjoy your smoke, Federico," Harper said in a good-humored tone. "Make sure you hide that lighter with the other item."

"What if he asks for it back?"

"Let's hope not," Harper replied, before transmitting more unsavory insults for the other inmate to lob at his jailer.

I wonder how long they'll keep this up? With luck, long enough for the guard to forget about his lighter.

NIGHT HAD COME. ALL THE INMATES WERE SLEEPING, SAVE FOR TWO.

Harper telepathed to Federico that it was time. Silently the Brazilian left his cot, removed the mattress, and picked up the purloined items. Firstly, a battery-operated driver, with the security bolt remover, he hung across his chest using torn-off strips of bedsheet as an improvised sling. Secondly, the guard's lighter he placed between his teeth.

The cell's cot-frame was placed on its end, the headboard allowed to rest against the wall. Apart from the occasional squeak of a bedspring, Federico noiselessly clambered up the makeshift ladder until he reached the ceiling bars. In next to no time, the security bolts removed, he had climbed through the access hatch.

Harper had been listening for any sound that would indicate the guard, who had cloistered himself in an empty cell at the other end of the block, had woken up and was on the move towards them.

The corridor remained empty.

All clear, Harper messaged inside Federico's head. *Pull your mattress through the ceiling bars and then step over here and take this one. Take care. Mine is heavy. I've already soaked it with water.*

Duty done, Federico moved to another four cells, quietly waking the inmates and collected their mattresses. In short order, he ripped open the casing and made a pile of the cotton wadding and coir fiber filling. Harper's mattress was placed on top, allowing the water to slowly soak into the dry material.

All set. Harper intercepted Federico's thought.

Let me check that Sleeping Beauty has not left his cell, Harper responded. Nothing moved at the far end. *Okay, all clear. Light it up, and get your sorry ass back down here ASAP.*

They only had to wait a couple of minutes before the damp wadding began producing clouds of choking smoke that percolated from the roof-space bonfire into the individual cells. The inmates were all banging on the steel bars with their mugs, rousing the guard from his slumber. With little time to summon help, the jailer hit the fire alarm and then began unlocking cells.

With satisfaction, Harper observed a steady stream of prisoners as they rushed past.

Then it was Federico's turn and finally his own. *In less than two dozen paces, we'll be free,* Harper thought.

Outside, he paused for an instant, sucking in the fresh, night air.

"Halt, immediately!" he heard someone shout over a bullhorn.

Suddenly his surroundings were lit up by a blaze of floodlights. Harper would have run except a cordon of armed soldiers blocked his path.

"Shit! How come they're this organized so quickly?"

"Nobody move!" the bullhorn commanded.

Instinctively Harper froze. Federico did the same. Both raised their hands in the air. Other escaping prisoners also complied.

Soldiers began moving forward, shaking out their collapsible batons. Harper's scheme was in ruins, but then it dawned on him that they were not going to shoot. Instead, they intended to corral the escapees and place them in another cellblock. The rest of the inmates must have reached the same conclusion for, as a force, they all rushed forward.

Weapons were drawn. Rifles and handguns were leveled at the detainees.

"Surrender, or you will be met with deadly force!" Bullhorn was at it again. Harper recognized the officer shouting orders as Captain Vickers. Vickers, he knew, was a man who did not like his sleep to be disrupted. Vickers preferred to spend his wake-time at the bar with a drink, not a pistol in his hand. In Harper's judgment, the Captain lacked the aptitude to make impromptu decisions. Furthermore, he did not have the ability to order his men to open fire because Vickers was a man not wearing a special foil-line helmet. Therefore, Vickers was susceptible to Harper planting suggestions inside his head.

"Men, stand down," the officer bellowed over the bullhorn.

The soldiers looked at each other, dumbfounded by what they thought to be a nonsensical order. A few complied. The majority, seeing Sergeant Johnson move towards the prisoners, raised their batons, and rushed forward.

Harper shouted, "Charge," as he sprinted into the mêlée. For what it was worth, Federico yelled the same directive in Portuguese, as he joined the brawl.

Fists are no match for batons unless there are enough of them. Prisoners outnumbered soldiers two to one. Rapidly the troops were overrun and surrendered. The game plan back on course, Harper started to dash towards the open gate of the compound.

"Stop, you American pig, or I kill you." Skidding to a halt and turning, Harper was now looking at the radical fanatic of his nightmares. If it had been a scene from *The Mummy* movie, the man might have been waving a khopesh. An Egyptian sickle-sword that evolved from battle-axes. But it was not. He was pointing a rifle, obtained by disarming one of the soldiers, at the American's chest.

Harper raised his hands. *You don't have to do this,* he suggested, telepathically venturing into his opponent's mind. *I am the messenger who spoke to you yesterday. I am the one who orchestrated your freedom. Put down your weapon.*

Hearing the bolt of the rifle being pulled back, the American tried talking instead, "Put the gun down. Nobody needs to die today."

برو به جهنم خود

Seeing a finger flex as the trigger was being squeezed, Harper decided now was not the best time to ask for a translation. Closing his eyes, his last thoughts were that of Jules, Oliver, and the baby. Perhaps if he had done things differently, he would have been allowed to be with them. Now that would never happen.

A sound like a sonic boom reached Harper's ears as a weapon discharged. He opened his eyes and stared at his mid-rift, expecting to see a bullet hole in his tunic. Then he looked toward the shooter, only to see the man crumple into a heap, blood oozing from the side of his head.

Federico grabbed Harper's arm as he shouted, "Come on. This way."

Together they ran from the spotlights and into the darkness. The American was so busy communicating telepathically with the soldiers, instructing them to stay put, he failed to notice Federico tossing a pistol away. Later he would learn the wannabe war correspondent had saved his life. However, their immediate objective was to leave as quickly as possible.

Thirty yards on, Harper abruptly stopped. "Hold up a minute, Federico. We're doing this all wrong."

"What do you mean?"

"We need to go back."

" Harper, are you mad? If we do, they will lock us up again."

"Maybe not," Harper replied. "I have an idea, which will keep these kooks off my back once and for all."

MANY ORGANIZATIONS HAVE AT LEAST ONE. GOING BY VARIOUS names such as fixer, sweeper, or cleaner, they clear up the messes, remove skeletons from closets, and ensure reputations remain unsullied. Unacknowledged, always ready and willing to do their Masters' bidding, they guarantee the unconscionable remains under wraps.

An American civilian, shot in the head during a prison escape was the sort of revelation to be avoided at all costs. However, with some adept maneuvering, the truth behind Harper's death could be covered up.

Except, of course, Harper was not dead. Notwithstanding, the staff at the Detention Camp believed he was, thanks to the American doubling back a few minutes after the rifle-toting Afghan was shot by Federico. Only those guards on duty in Harper's cellblock wore the foil-lined helmets. Everyone else was vulnerable to Harper getting inside their minds and changing their perceptions. All he had to do was take advantage as pandemonium reigned during the escapees' roundup. Crouched behind a fire truck, the American was able to make everyone believe he was the victim lying dead on the ground.

The only potential fly in the ointment would be Kirt Mitchell. Should he look at the corpse, sharing the same mental abilities, there was no way Harper could control the man's cognizance. Fortunately, Midnight was tucked up in bed in the Officers' Quarters, sleeping off the drinking session he had indulged himself in a few hours before.

The body remained covered by a tarp until Sergeant Johnson arrived on the scene. Assisted by a second cleaner, what was believed to be Harper's body was taken back into the smoke-damaged detention block and placed in a cell away from the entrance. The adjacent corridor was filled with mattresses. Once the fire was lit, the pair retreated a safe distance to enjoy the bonfire. They were unaware that the American was controlling their minds throughout their nefarious endeavor, thus ensuring the dead Afghan's identity was not revealed.

The next day a charred corpse was taken to the Base morgue, where it remained, without a postmortem, until it was covertly shipped to the mainland for cremation.

In the meantime, the alive-and-kicking Harper was free to roam the forty-five square miles of land leased from the Cuban Government, established under the treaty of 1903.

Anyone he came across ignored the stranger dressed in army fatigues. The American was able to enter the barracks, shower, shave, and change clothes without being challenged. He ate at the mess hall and slept in a comfortable bed. Like a fly on the wall, Harper was privy to their idle chitchat, picking up one snippet in particular that all the escapees except one had been rounded up. Nobody asked any questions. Nobody challenged his presence. To them, he was a nondescript soldier taking some R&R.

All that was left to do was gather necessary supplies and then choose the right moment to walk through to the Northeast Gate, once an entry point for Cuban dayworkers. From there, he and Federico would have access to the rest of the island. Only one problem; the gate was padlocked.

HAVING RECONNOITERED THEIR PROPOSED EXIT EARLIER THAT DAY, Harper had also ascertained the key was kept on a hook inside the small security hut adjacent to the Northeast Gate. No big deal. Having done it many times before, the escapee had casually sauntered up to his objective, and by accessing the guards' minds made them believe he was not there.

Rather than just taking the key, he molded three sticks of chewing gum into a block big enough to take an impression of the bit. Then he placed the key back on the hook, not wanting to raise any speculation should it be found missing.

Wearing a clean military uniform, borrowed from an unsuspecting corporal's locker, it was a no-brainer to visit the Navy Exchange store off of Sherman Avenue and get a key cut that would fit the padlock. Harper also purchased a can of WD-40, a couple of stainless steel vacuum flasks, an off-the-peg lightweight cotton suit, a selection of shirts, underwear, socks, and a pair of shoes. He made a similar selection for Federico, subsisting a denim jacket and jeans as the alternative to a suit. He decided to skip shoes for his Brazilian friend and purchased a pair of hiking boots instead.

Shopping finished, Harper made his way to the Subway®

restaurant, which was next door, and stuffed himself with a chicken and bacon submarine sandwich. Not forgetting his partner in crime, he chose a steak and cheese wrap to-go.

"Andy!" Lance Corporal Grover, inside the security hut, shouted to his colleague.

With his iPod blasting reggae music through a pair of earbuds, Andy took no notice.

For a second time, the lance corporal tried to get Andy's attention. Only when tapped on the shoulder, did he receive a response. "What now, Grover? You're not going to tell me another of your corny jokes, are you?"

"No. I thought I heard something outside. Listen."

Andy reluctantly turned off the music and removed his earbuds. "You mean the sound of crickets, I presume."

"Not that. A squeaking sound."

"Grover, go back to your book, and stop bothering me."

"There it is again. Maybe someone's trying to get in?"

"Whatever for?" Andy asked.

"I don't know. Steal a battleship, maybe?"

"Ha, ha; very funny."

"I'm going to check."

"Suit yourself, Grover. I'm going back to Bob Marley."

Harper was not into Bob Marley. He was too busy heading west, scurrying along the exterior road that ran parallel with the camp's boundary fence. Having chosen a moonless night, he could hear the sound of Federico's footsteps crunching the gravel five yards in front of him. They continued for fifteen minutes before stopping at the point where their projected route started the lazy arc of a turn to the north.

ONCE HE HAD CAUGHT HIS BREATH, FEDERICO ASKED, "WHY ALL
the panic? I don't see any guards racing after us."

"And hopefully, you won't, my friend," Harper replied. "I guess I
overreacted."

Twenty minutes earlier, Harper and Federico had stealthily skirted
the security hut, keeping low as they approached the Northeast Gate
of the camp. They could see the two guards, both of whom seemed
preoccupied with their own business, neither one looking through
the hut's windows. Which was good, Harper decided, for he had his
hands full constraining Federico from running directly up to the gate
and attempting to climb over. The razor wire on the top, he had to
explain, was something to be taken seriously.

Reaching the gate itself without incident, he pulled the can of
WD-40 from a purloined knapsack and prudently oiled the padlock.
Putting the recently made key into the lock, he prayed it would turn
without a problem. Although he had brought a small hand-file to

make minor adjustments to the key, it was not necessary. His prayer was answered.

Silently removing the chain, he gently pushed on one side of the double gate.

`Squ-ea-k!`

Darn it, Harper cursed to himself, having forgotten to oil the hinges. *Too late now*, he concluded. After hustling Federico through the small gap, the American followed.

Squ-ea-k!

Double darn.

Once closed, Harper hurriedly wrapped the chain back around the double gates, re-applied the padlock, and quickly turned the key. It was then that one of the sentries stood up, placed an object on a table, and started heading towards the door of the hut.

Move! Harper instilled the instruction into his companion's mind. *Run, Federico, as fast as you can. I think one of the guards is about to visit us.*

"Was that Rafael at the gate with the box of Cuban cigars I'd ordered?" Andy inquired as Grover returned.

"You're quite the comedian this evening, it seems. Nobody was there. Strange thing, though. Someone recently oiled the padlock."

"Not so much," Andy contradicted. "It just means some officer has their head screwed on straight. What good would it do if we had to open the gate in a rush, only to find the key wouldn't turn in the padlock?"

There was a pause. Grover sat down, but instead of returning to his book, he chose to gaze out of the window.

"What's the problem now, Champ?"

"Nothing. I thought I saw someone running along the fence line; that's all."

"You know, Grover, you take this job far too seriously. Give us all a break, and go back to your reading."

"I've nearly finished. D'you want to borrow it when I'm done?"

"Depends. What's it called?" Andy asked.

"*The Great Escape* by Paul Brickhill."

"Nah. But thanks anyway. I've seen the movie. Do you remember how Steve McQueen jumped the fence on a motorcycle? That sure was something."

10

Without a motorcycle to ride, some two hours later, Harper and Federico sat down by the roadside to rest. Apart from the occasional lights of fishing boats in the bay, they had seen nothing of interest

The Brazilian removed his boots and socks. "I have a blister on my heel."

"Let me see," Harper said in response. "That looks ugly."

"Feels ugly too." Federico pulled back the top layer of broken skin. "It's your fault, Harper. You should have got me some sandals."

"I was trying to be helpful, that's all. As a war correspondent, you should be accustomed to wearing them."

"But not after I've been a prisoner issued with canvas footwear, Harper. Do you have anything in that backpack of yours to treat the broken skin?"

"Some antiseptic ointment and a selection of Band-Aids. Here. Help yourself." Harper tossed a first aid kit in the Brazilian's direction.

Once Federico's self-doctoring was done, Harper pulled a map from his inside jacket pocket and tried to decide exactly where they were. "I think we're here," he concluded, pointing.

Federico laughed. "You wish, Harper. If you were right, we would have been walking at … Let me think." After a quick calculation, he continued, "six kilometers per hour. Taking into account the rest-stops we made, we are more likely to have averaged four kilometers per hour."

"Enough of this metric stuff, Federico? Just show me exactly where we are."

Having determined they were southeast of *Guantánamo* city, a further fourteen miles by road, Harper suggested they lay low until daybreak, eat some of their provisions, and get some sleep. Federico was not going to argue, as his legs ached from the unaccustomed forced exercise. Having found a cluster of boulders to protect him from the wind, the Brazilian checked for scorpions and snakes before lying down.

No sooner had he drifted off, it seemed the American was shaking him awake.

"Leave me alone, Harper, and let me get some rest."

"You've had your rest. You've slept like a baby for three hours. The sun will be up any minute. Grab a snack and some water, and get ready to move."

It was not long before Federico started complaining once more about his aching legs. Unsympathetically, Harper suggested they call a taxi, punctuating his inane comment by stating, "Oh, silly me. I forgot my cell phone."

"I should have stayed in the camp," Federico concluded. "At least there, we were caged in separate cells."

"*Caged* is the operative word, my Brazilian friend. But don't let me stop you. Feel free to go right on back and turn yourself in."

"Returning to the camp is almost a far as continuing to the town of *Guantánamo*. I think I will stay with you."

"That's the spirit," Harper replied. "You never know, we might get lucky and hitch a ride."

Federico scowled and concentrated on placing one foot in front of the other. Nothing was said between them for the next twenty minutes as the sun began to warm their backs. Nothing that is until Federico stopped suddenly in his tracks and turned around.

"Blessed Virgin Mary; my prayers are answered."

The American also stopped and turned. "Whatever are you talking about, Federico?"

His companion did not have to answer, for coming over the rise was a dilapidated pickup truck that Henry Ford might have built himself.

This should be good, Harper told himself, as Federico stepped into the vehicle's path and frantically began waving his arms. *The chances of a Brazilian and a Cuban successfully conversing in sign language is practically zero.*

To the American's astonishment, once the driver stopped and rolled down his window, Federico began holding a frenzied conversation in Spanish. *Of course, you told me you had friends on the island. You're fluent in Spanish as well as English and Portuguese. I wonder what other things you're good at that will help me get out of this accursed mess?*

"WHAT DID YOU SAY TO THE CUBAN THAT PERSUADED HIM TO GIVE us a lift?" Harper asked Federico as they sat in the flatbed of the truck, which jarred their backs whenever the wheels found a pothole.

Federico laughed. "I told him you and I had met in Havana, and that you had come up with this harebrained scheme to smuggle Cuban cigars onto the base in exchange for a truckload of DVDs."

"Hmm," Harper responded dubiously. "And that accounts for us being on foot in the middle of nowhere?"

"I told him we met your contact at the boundary fence and were making the exchange when a patrol showed up in a Humvee. The next thing we knew, they were shooting at us. Our vehicle had its tires blown out, and we had to make a run for it."

"Full marks for imagination, Federico. You should have been a writer. Why did you give him the bars of chocolate?"

"I saw them in your sack. In order to make the story believable, I told him the only things we came away with were a few Hershey Bars. He said his kids loved American chocolate. I think that was the deal clincher. Good job, he did not ask for a box of cigars."

It was Harper's turn to laugh. "If you must know, I've got a couple tucked away in my pocket. Do you want a smoke?"

Federico shook his head, turning his attention to the scenery, grateful to be out off the dreadful prison cell.

The pickup bounced in and out of one more pothole, and the American was thrown to the side. The cuff of his jacket was now stained a dirty brown color. He tried to rub it off.

"Leave it alone, Harper. Walking around in a freshly pressed suit is going to make people wonder. I do not expect there are many dry cleaners in these parts."

"You're probably right, Federico," the American agreed. "Did you find out where we're headed?"

"Right where we need to be, Guantánamo city. Today is market day."

"Then, you're prayers were truly answered, my friend. We'll hop a bus or train and be in Havana in no time."

"That's where you're wrong, Harper," Federico responded. "It is approximately seven hundred and fifty kilometers to the capital. It will take at fifteen or so hours."

An airplane could be seen circling for a landing to the northwest.

"Then we should take a plane ride." the American declared.

"You have enough money?" Federico asked.

"I *acquired* almost three hundred American dollars during my trips to the barracks and shopping malls," Harper whispered as if it should remain a secret between them.

The truck found another pothole, resulting in more dirt soiling Harper's clothing.

"So your plan is to charter a plane. That is bound to arouse suspicion."

"Why should it?" Harper responded nonchalantly. "I'll tell them we're a couple of tourists who got separated from our coach party."

"And they will believe you?" Federico asked.

"Don't see why not? What do you think?" Harper inquired of the goat that was tied up next to him.

"Me-eh-eh-eh," the animal answered.

"My thoughts exactly," Federico concurred.

As they left the pickup, Federico asked the driver if he had any idea the price of the airfare to Havana. When told a charter might cost the equivalent of a thousand dollars, the pair were forced to seek an alternative. They found the railway station but noticed a member of the *Policía Nacional Revolucionaria* checking everyone's ticket. Not taking any chances, Harper elected to head for the bus station.

Once there, they joined the line at the *Astro* ticket office. As Harper waited, he glanced at their prospective mode of transport, which was belching black smoke as it idled its engine. He groaned to himself when he realized it was not air-conditioned. His misery was compounded when he saw the driver kicking the balding tires as if that was safety inspection enough.

"We cannot stay here." Harper swiveled around, hearing the Brazilian's whispered voice, as he approached from behind.

"Why not, Federico; what's wrong?"

"You recall the policeman at the railway station. There are more here, checking passengers as they board the bus. I think the Naval Base has alerted the Cuban authorities after finally realizing that I am missing."

"I didn't think America was talking to the Cuban authorities," Harper countered.

"Evidently, they are. Must be a spinoff from the détente established during the Obama administration. Don't you read the newspapers, Harper?"

"I try not too," Harper responded with a grin. "I leave that to journalists like yourself." As the pair broke away from the line of people queuing for tickets, he continued, "So what do we do now, Federico? As you said, it's a long way to the capital, and I don't feel like walking."

"Remember, I told you I have friends on the island," Federico responded. "Well, one of them is rather special. Before I went to Afghanistan, she was my girlfriend. Her parents happened to live in a small village not far from here. Maybe I can persuade them to loan us a vehicle?"

"It's worth a try," Harper agreed. "A moment ago, you said she *was* your girlfriend. Does that mean one of you broke it off?"

"I'm not sure," Federico replied sheepishly. "Problem is, I left the country and forgot to tell her where I was going."

Harper laughed.

"What is so funny? She probably thinks I dumped her."

"That's one way of putting it," Harper replied, unsympathetically. "Remind me, Federico, never to employ you as my social secretary. Can you remember her name, or is that something else you've forgotten?"

THE SUN, NOW HIGH IN THE SKY, MADE THE TREK WEARISOME. Harper mopped his brow with a handkerchief as a dump truck slowed for a moment only to pick up speed and pass them by.

"That's the third vehicle to do that," the American remarked. "What is it that makes the people around here so unfriendly?"

"You," Federico replied. "They see you're wearing a suit."

"Every truck driver has an opinion about the latest fashion, is that it?" Harper responded indignantly. "What do they expect? Beachwear, I suppose."

"It's not that, Harper. Cubans, in general, dress casually. Men, in particular, don't wear suits, especially in the countryside. They are just a little suspicious, that's all. Don't take it personally."

The American huffed in response, removing his jacket, hoping the next vehicle would stop.

To their left, they heard the sound of banging as maintenance workers readied a sugar mill for the harvest, which Cubans called *zafra*.

"How much further?" the American asked as the frequency of dwellings increased.

"Not far," Federico replied. "A few hundred meters past the baseball field."

"It's too hot for baseball." The American ran his fingers through his thinning hair, wishing he were wearing a baseball cap. "It's too hot for anything. I'm exhausted."

"It was your idea to leave the comforts of your prison cell, Harper. Stop complaining. Come on; we'll soon be there."

As a distraction from the long walk, the American asked his companion what he previously did in Cuba.

"Before my enforced stay at Gitmo, you mean? I was a freelance reporter with the Associated Press, living in Havana. I used to send in copy two or three times a month. More often, if there was something of international interest going on. That reminds me, as soon as I get to the city, I need to give them a call. Maybe, I can get my old job back?"

"Hardly a full-time occupation, though," Harper assumed. "What else did you do with your time?"

"I had a good time, enjoyed a few beers; that sort of thing," The Brazilian replied.

"Federico, you look like an educated individual. I sense there is more to your life than that."

"You're right," the Brazilian confessed. "The prime reason I came to Cuba was a fact-finding expedition, to enable me to write a biography on the infamous *Presidente* Fulgencio Batista."

"A strange choice, if you ask me," Harper commented. "Why Batista in particular?"

"Because he was wrapped up in a conspiracy."

"A conspiracy to defraud the Cuban people of millions of dollars of what should have been their money."

"No. Something else," Federico countered.

"Aren't you going to tell me what?" the American asked.

"Nope," was the curt reply. "You'll have to wait and read the book."

A sultry lady in her mid-twenties, with raven hair that flowed down her back, answered the door of a single-story house sadly in need of some TLC. Quickly getting over her surprise, after seeing Federico, she entered into a lengthy tirade, delivered in Spanish at breakneck speed. When finally finished, she followed up by smacking the Brazilian firmly across the face.

The girlfriend, Harper assumed, smiling weakly in the woman's direction. The air was filled with hostility.

Federico broke the standoff by offering introductions. "Karmina, this is Harper; Harper, say hello to Karmina."

Karmina glowered at the American, clearly indicating that a friend of Federico was no friend of hers.

"Pleased to meet you, Karmina," Harper responded timidly. "Your boyfriend has been through what can only be described as a terrible ordeal in prison."

"Prisión?" For the second time, Karmina expressed surprise. Turning her head to face the Brazilian, she asked, "*¿Has sido encerrado en prisión?* [You've been locked up in prison?]" Federico nodded. "*Mi pobre bebé* [My poor baby]." With that, she began smothering him with kisses.

It would seem the happy couple is back together again. I wonder if I should add matchmaker to my résumé? Harper asked himself.

14

HAVING LEFT HER PARENTS HOME, HEADING FOR HAVANA, KARMINA was driving her boxy Lada sedan, circa 1980. She seemed oblivious of the blue plume of smoke that belched endlessly from the exhaust, indicating the engine was burning oil.

"So tell me; how did you boys meet up?" Karmina asked in English, having been told that the American did not speak Spanish.

Harper, who was sitting in the back, this time without chickens or a goat, spoke first, offering Federico some friendly words of wisdom. "Best tell the truth, old buddy. You're lucky to have escaped the doghouse, so don't push your luck with a fabricated story."

For thirty minutes, wide-eyed, Karmina listed to how the pair were guests at the Hotel Guantánamo, courtesy of the US Government.

The majority of other vehicles streamed past, many exceeding *el límite de velocidad de la autopista* [the freeway's speed limit]. The Lada struggled to maintain a steady forty-five miles per hour. Buffeted by the wind, the vehicle rattled and squeaked as the shock absorbers protested at their unaccustomed payload.

Eventually, the conversation moved away from the detention

camp. Federico asked Harper what he did for a living when he wasn't playing at being a prison inmate, that is.

"I take care of other people's money," the American replied, which, in a sense, was true, having relieved Kirt Mitchell of his share of the poker winnings, and depleted the offshore bank accounts, through a mind-meld, of his nemesis Geoffrey Phelps. The later bankrolled the medical research that Harper had been subjected to years earlier.

"A banker, hah. Not my idea of a profession," the Brazilian decided. "I prefer the outdoors and to work freelance. Still, every man to his own taste."

"I get out and about," Harper countered.

For example, the time spent in captivity on a converted oil platform in the Gulf of Mexico, and choosing to live in the UAE. The latter a convenient means of avoiding extradition to the USA for two alleged murders. Those last two thoughts he kept to himself, choosing, for the moment, to lapse into silence.

Making good time, they joined *Carretera Central*, or Highway 1, and continued heading west. Passing clusters of trees on their right and one-story detached homes on their left, the latter reminded Harper of a spread-out trailer park.

"You know, *mi amigo*," Federico announced, "something in your story doesn't quite jell. Tell me; how does a banker end up getting recruited to interrogate prisoners? That's what you told me when we first spoke."

"In truth, I was never a banker, Federico. You're very astute if I may say so."

"Comes with the territory of being a newshound. A great asset if one is sniffing out a story. And I think you have a story, Mr. Harper. Am I right?"

"Harper, please. Just call me Harper."

15

Throwing caution to the wind, Harper began his narrative.

Starting with his service as an army sniper out of Fort Benning, he told how he got to know a girl named Christina Martinez, how they became engaged, and the tragedy of her death when their vehicle was T-boned by another car running a red light. Harper ended up hospitalized, the first three months in a coma.

The American left out of his account any reference to his receiving a course of drugs administered by two doctors who were endeavoring to enhance their subject's brainpower.

Harper went on to tell, once he was released from the hospital, that he was unable to cope with his fiancée's death. He became violent and disorderly, which resulted in him receiving a dishonorable discharge from the army. Life continued in a downward spiral, with Harper aimlessly drifting from bar to bar, trying to forget.

The low point was when he contemplated suicide. About to jump off a bridge, a stranger, whose name was Kirt Mitchell, intervened. After talking him down, the stranger discovered Harper had a *natural ability* when playing poker. Mitchell was a gambler, who saw an opportunity to stack the odds in his favor if they worked as a team. Together, they hatched a scheme to win at a major poker tournament.

Of course, Harper's *not so natural* ability was reading minds. Telepathically communicating back and forth, once Mitchel knew the other players' cards, he told Harper when to bet and when to fold. Their strategy succeeded big time, netting over ten million dollars. Notwithstanding, Mitchell intended to keep the proceeds all to himself, by arranging for Harper to be drugged with a tranquilizing sedative, then abducted by helicopter to a pod of modified oil rigs in the Gulf of Mexico, there to be imprisoned.

Harper soon discovered the same two doctors who had experimented on him years before ran the complex, in absentia. There he met Julia Norton, who was being forced to provide medical care for the kidnapped prisoners on the rigs.

Just as the American had broken out of Camp Five Echo, he had hatched a plot to free himself from the Gulf of Mexico prison. After calling in a debt from a fixed poker game, he, Julia, and a small group of inmates were rescued in a submarine by a retired British admiral.

"Subsequently, Julia and I got married, set up house in Dubai, raised our son, Oliver, and lived happily ever after."

"You didn't go back to the USA?" Federico asked when the American paused in his commentary.

"Yes, but I left in a rush, soon after," Harper replied. "Turns out, the FBI wanted me for an alleged murder."

"Which you didn't commit?"

"No, but they all say that, don't they?" Not elaborating further, the American resorted to a pathetic wimp of a laugh.

There was silence for a time. Karmina concentrated on her driving. Federico gazed out of the side window, leaving Harper wondering what Julia and Oliver were doing.

It was Karmina who spoke next. "So what made you leave Dubai, and how come you ended up in Cuba?"

"Another long story," Harper replied.

"We're listening," Federico told him. "It's still a long way to Havana."

HARPER, REALIZING TO PROTEST WAS POINTLESS, CONTINUED, "While living in Dubai, I was approached by the son of the British Admiral who rescued me from the ocean prison. Small world, you'll agree. Anyway, it turned out the Admiral's son was a Colonel in the British Security Service, MI5. He recruited me to help investigate a mysterious epidemic that was infecting groups of people with a strain of *Caseous lymphadenitis,* usually found only sheep and goats. The Colonel believed the outbreak might have been a deliberate act of bioterrorism."

"Sounds like something I'd like to get my teeth into, as a journalist that is," Federico chipped in.

Harper resumed his story. "It turned out, the company that was manufacturing a vaccine for the Government was owned by none other than the two doctors who experimented on me in the States."

"A small world, indeed," Federico remarked, repeating the American's words.

Harper smiled. Much like his own, he liked the Brazilian's sense of humor.

"It turned out to be part of an elaborate ruse, in two ways. Firstly the two doctors managed to extract payment from the

National Health Service, and all they were manufacturing were vials of sugar water reinforced with vitamins. Furthermore, the disease was not contagious at all, being transmitted by nasal spray to the victims."

"Wish I had my tape recorder with me, Harper," Federico commented. "Wait a second." The Brazilian delved into the Lada's glove box. "Here we are; pen and paper. Do you mind if I make some notes?"

"No note-taking, Federico. It is all classified. And you did promise not to put any of this in a novel."

"If it's classified, Harper, why are you telling us this?"

"Good question," the American replied. "Perhaps I should stop?"

"Please don't," Karmina implored. "It's just getting interesting."

"And I'm waiting to hear, what was this second ruse?" the Brazilian asked.

"One of the doctors, named Hyde, was plotting to loot many of the nation's paintings from London's art galleries. He did this by releasing a deadly gas that knocked out many of the capital's citizens. The theft succeeds too. It took my expertise to track down the stolen items and facilitate their recovery."

"Just like Sherlock Holmes would have done," Karmina concluded.

"Something like that," Harper agreed.

"Are you and Sherlock related?" was her next question.

"Could be, Karmina." Harper added drolly, "On my mother's side, I believe."

Harper laughed at his own joke. Anything to keep Federico and Karmina for uncovering his true abilities.

IT WAS THE EARLY HOURS OF THE MORNING WHEN THEY REACHED
the outskirts of Havana. Nevertheless, the nightlife in such a vibrant
city was still in full swing. The nearer they got to the waterfront, the
more congested the traffic became. Harper was fascinated by the
collection of old cars, all in pristine condition, that would have been
given pride of place in any American auto museum.

Despite the multitude of vehicles and jaywalking pedestrians,
Karmina deftly wove in and out of the bustle, aided by the liberal
use of the horn and the occasional unladylike expletive or flip of the
finger.

Eventually, they turned east into *Calle Acosta*, finally stopping
when they reached the small square at the corner of *San Ignacio*.
Karmina turned off the car's ignition and led the way to the third
floor of a four-story building, built in the colonial style.

The apartment she rented was a shoebox by American
standards. Three hundred and twenty square feet in total, the area
was divided between a tiny kitchen, a living room, one bedroom,
and a bathroom, the latter with the most grotesque pink tiling
Harper had ever seen.

Karmina invited her guests to sit on the couch while she went into the kitchen, pulled two cans of locally brewed *Mayabe* lager, and a bottle of water from the refrigerator. Harper and Federico took the beers. After perching herself on the desk in the corner of the room, Karmina picked up on the unfinished story by asking Harper, "You never said why you left Britain and came here."

"Dictates of the job," the American replied in an off-hand manner. Not wanting to elaborate, he added, "That too is classified. I can't say more."

"All this is a ploy, Harper. You are CIA," Federico declared, "secretly infiltrating Cuba."

"The card games, the oil platform prison, and me helping the British Government; they're all true, I swear," Harper insisted.

"If you say so, Harper," the Brazilian responded. "That still doesn't eliminate you as being CIA." Turning his head toward Karmina, he offered a sly smile and said, "The plot thickens, Watson; that's what Holmes would say."

"I don't think so," his girlfriend replied. "I believe the phrase is *the game is afoot*. Am I right, Harper?"

"I must confess, I'm more of a Hercule Poirot fan myself," Harper confided, "so if you two will excuse me, it's time I got some shut-eye. I am going to sleep here on the couch. You two can argue about which side of the bed you want to sleep. It *is* a double, I presume?"

Unceremoniously, the American push Federico out of the way and settle down for the rest of the night.

By the time everyone had showered and dressed, it was almost noon. Federico suggested that they eat brunch at a café on the next block, which had sidewalk seating and offered all the ambiance of a five-star Cuban restaurant without the price tag.

They were lucky to get a table. The majority of patrons were local, with a smattering of foreigners who had strayed from the tourist hotspots.

Coffee and *tostones* were the order of the day. All three bit into the flattened pieces of crispy-fried plantain, after dunking them into the accompanying chocolate dip.

Harper felt the hot breeze on his face, which perversely reminded him of the detention camp and all its unpleasant connotations. Notwithstanding, happy to be free, he asked, "Federico, tell me more about your research into Fulgencio Batista. You implied it poses somewhat of an enigma."

"Shush, Harper," the Brazilian admonished. "Lower your voice. People can hear you."

The American pulled a face as if the rebuff had hurt his feelings. "Come on, Federico. How many years has it been since the Revolution?"

"I am serious. Many people still harbor hatred for the man. If they think you are a sympathizer, you could end up in jail."

"I only mentioned his name. That hardly makes me a sympathizer. How about we whisper?"

"It's no joke, Harper. Best only to speak of these things when we are back in the apartment."

"Whatever," the American replied, dismissively. "These *tostones* are rather good. Almost beats a Kentucky fried chicken. What's your opinion, Karmina?"

"Be quiet, Harper. People are looking at you."

THE SUN HAD MOVED OFF THE FRONT OF THE BUILDING. DESPITE THE apartment's louvered shutters, without air conditioning or a fan, for the American, the heat had become unbearable. Neither Federico nor Karmina seemed to mind. Harper, despite the time he had spent in an oppressive prison cell, yearned of the comforts of his beachside villa in Dubai. He would even settle for the drafty castle where he had resided for a few weeks, while in England. At least the place was cooler. However, it was what it was. The Brazilian had asked for his help, so he listened patiently to what was being said.

Federico punctuated his sentences by frantically waving a leather-bound book in front of himself.

During his research, the Brazilian had spent time reading newspaper articles alluding to events that lead to Castro taking control of the county. He had come across an article clipped from the Cuban newspaper *El Tiempo*, dated April 20th, 1957, that told of a shootout at an apartment building in Humboldt Street, where six members of the *Directorio Revolucionario* were hiding. *Captán* Ventura was credited as being the mastermind behind the police raid.

Later, the journalist had visited several flea and street markets in the city, searching for books or other items that were connected with the years before the Revolution.

By chance, the Brazilian's own words, he had come across a selection of personal belongings acquired from a house clearance following the death of the owner. Included, there was an assortment of scrapbooks and photo albums. As Federico slowly thumbed through each album, he saw family groups. One member, in particular, looked familiar. Turning the page, he saw the same person, this time dressed in the uniform of a Captain of police. It was the very man featured in the newspaper article; Esteban Ventura, who served in President Batista's regime.

The Brazilian also discovered a diary, kept by the police Captain containing entries beginning in 1951 and continuing until his death in 1987. The journal, previously bequeathed to his son, was now part of a growing pile of items that the reporter intended to purchase.

Some of the entries were detailed, while others were no more than a line or two. There were references to the time Ventura was arrested by the Revolutionary Government, comments on the executions of some of Batista's henchmen, and the time the former policeman spent in prison for crimes against the people.

Harper had taken a cursory look inside, but being written in Spanish, he handed the book back to the Brazilian who translated sections of the text as he proceeded with his commentary.

One account referred to January 1st, 1959, the day before Batista made a hurried exit by airplane to *Ciudad Trujillo*, in the Dominican Republic. As a parting gift, the fleeing President gave Ventura a carriage clock. A strange present one might have thought until further reading revealed the back of the clock was a receptacle for a key, which opened a lower draw in an early 19th century Southern American library bookcase. The former police Captain had annotated a discussion he had had with one of the servants. Every day from May 1953 until the end of December 1958, Batista had opened the said drawer, peeked inside, before locking it again.

Neither Ventura nor the servant knew what the President hoped to find. However, the man's frustration was frequently vented using the phrases *Vamos, Carlos, estoy esperando* [Come on, Carlos, I am waiting], *¿Qué te está llevando tanto tiempo, Fuentes?* [What is taking you so long, Fuentes?], or variations of the same.

"Interesting," Harper said, "assuming *El Presidente* is not an obsessive-compulsive, that is. It would surely add some color to the biography if you could find out what he was expecting to be in that drawer."

"Precisely. And that's where you come in, Harper. I was hoping you would help me retrieve the clock."

"You know where it is?" the American asked, captivated by the enigma.

"I am not one hundred percent certain, but before I become a war correspondent, I had a possible lead. The stallholder told me that some jewelry, a clock, and a selection of silver-plated picture frames had been snapped up by, a *señor* Pallares, the owner of an antique shop in *Vedado*. I followed up by visiting the place. However, when I mentioned a carriage clock, *señor* Pallares became evasive, denying he had acquired one recently."

"After all this time, you think I'll have more success?" Harper asked doubtfully.

"Posing as an American tourist, Harper, yes. Especially if you start waving banknotes under his nose."

"Okay. I'll give it a try. On one condition."

"Name it, Harper. Just name it."

"As soon as you have this clock in your possession, you help me get off the island."

"Done and done." Federico sounded like a kid on a day when Santa Claus had come early.

HARPER WAS LOOKING FOR A SHOP ON *CALLE 33*. IN DUE COURSE, HE found it on the corner of *Calle 4*. Formerly a house, the ground floor front room had been converted by adding a window that displayed a collection of antiques, bric-a-brac, and novelty souvenirs. Overhead, in peeling green lettering, were the words, **ANTIGÜEDADES PALLARES**.

Deciding this was the place Federico had described, he tried the door. It was locked. A reversible sign read ***CERRADO.*** Closed, Harper assumed. Too early to be lunchtime, he wondered why the shop was not open for business.

He put his face to the glass and squinted inside. He could see a lamp burning in the back room. The American rapped hard on the door with his knuckles.

No response.

He tried again, harder this time, but still, no answer.

Again, looking through the glass, he could see someone had turned off the light.

He wrapped once more. The result was the same. Deciding there was little point in continuing, he turned to leave.

After taking three paces, Harper stopped. Walking back to the door, he stood outside, closed his eyes, and concentrated.

Déjanos en paz. ¿No ves que estamos cerrados?

Spanish. What was the person thinking? *Cerrados.* Whatever it was, it amounted to the same thing; *closed.*

Why?

Harper hoped the man or woman inside spoke English. Telepathically he transmitted, *Hello. Please open the door. I am an American tourist. I want to buy some antiques.*

"Go away," was the barely audible response. "We are not open for business." Of course, Harper was not relying on voice. He understood the speaker's thoughts.

I've come a long way. I want to buy one of your clocks.

There was a shuffling sound as someone moved towards the door. A stocky, round-faced man looked out. "The sign says closed. Come back another time."

"I'm leaving Cuba tomorrow," Harper replied, in the hope the speaker would change his mind. "I collect clocks. A friend of mine saw one in your shop some time ago that he thinks would interest me."

The face on the other side of the glass turned back towards the room.

"I pay well," Harper shouted, waving a wad of twenty-dollar bills that he held in his hand.

Money does not just talk; it swears. Unable to resist, no matter the reason to lock his door, the proprietor let the American inside.

Once the door had been relocked and introductions were completed, the owner asked, "A clock you say; what type, exactly?"

"A carriage clock. I have a collection of fifty or so at my home in New York."

"I have only three, as you can see." The proprietor, who wore a threadbare jacket patched at the elbows, waved his arm in the direction of a showcase set along the right-hand wall.

Harper walked over, pulled a photograph from his suit jacket, which the Brazilian had found in one of the albums, and compared the picture with those on display. None matched.

Returning to the counter, the American handed Pallares the photograph. The clock casing, a bronzed caramel metallic color, was approximately six inches tall, by six inches wide. The depth was about an inch. A handle on the top resembled the shape of the letter F. The dial consisted of black Roman numerals, interspaced with single fleur-de-lis motifs, while the hour and minute hands lacked any adornment. Small raised rosettes and overelaborate filigree were equally spaced around the circumference of the glass, a concession to an otherwise nondescript appearance.

"Umm. Not the usual design for a carriage clock. I am afraid I have nothing like this on display, *señor*."

Not on display. Perhaps in the back room?

Harper, in mind-probing mode, had slipped a thought into the proprietor's head, which resulted in Pallares asking, "You said you are a collector. Out of interest, tell me, what is the most prized exhibit you have acquired?"

"Let me think." The American creased his forehead in mock concentration. "It's got to be an Abraham-Louis Breguet clock similar to the one made for the French Emperor Napoleon in 1812. I paid," Harper pulled a number out of the top of his head, "$40,000 at auction."

Pallares asked, full of anticipation, "The clock you are seeking, the one in this photograph, is that worth as much?"

"Hardly. It lacks the sophistication of the French clockmaker. However, I am interested because it is similar to one owned by my grandfather. Sold in a garage sale many years ago, I was told. Finding one similar would bring back fond memories."

Pallares scratched his bald head. "Assuming I could put my hands on such a clock, how much would you pay?"

With an inner satisfaction, *the fish is on the hook*, Harper thought to himself. "How does fifteen hundred dollars sound?"

"American dollars, *señor?*"

"Is there any other kind?" Harper replied with a grin, slowly flicking through his wad of bills.

20

INSIDE THE APARTMENT, KARMINA, WHO CONSIDERED HERSELF mechanically minded, sat at the desk, shining a small flashlight inside the carriage clock's gearing. She had inserted the key, wound up the spring, and was trying to figure out why the clock was not working.

Meanwhile, over on the couch, Federico was quizzing Harper as to how he managed to *acquire* the timepiece.

"I offered him fifteen hundred dollars," was the American's response.

"But you do not have fifteen hundred dollars," the Brazilian replied, looking confused.

In a conspiratorial manner, Harper lowered his voice. "Don't tell *señor* Pallares that. I counted out *fifteen* bills. Only the top and bottom were one-hundreds. Those in the middle were twenties. The greedy antique shop owner never thought to check closely."

"You can do things like that?" the Brazilian exclaimed.

"Between ourselves, Federico, sleight of hand has been my party trick ever since I learned to play cards," Harper replied in a hushed voice.

"Your secret is safe with me, *amigo*," the Brazilian confided in an equally subdued manner.

"What are you two whispering about over there?" Karmina asked, looking up from her unsuccessful attempt to free the spring with a small screwdriver.

"Harper was telling me how easy it was to persuade Pallares to part with the clock. Once he saw the color of his money, he miraculously remembered he had it out back," Federico answered, in Spanish.

"Well, don't get too pleased with yourselves. For a start, the damn thing does not work. And there is no second key that might fit a lock to a bureau drawer."

Harper walked over to the desk. "Let me take a look, Karmina."

Picking up the clock, he took it to the open window where there was more light. After opening the back and squinting inside, he tugged on the carrying handle. To his surprise, the lid came off.

"Well, I never," the American declared. "Would you two look at this?"

He was holding up another key that had been jammed inside the mechanism.

"I think we're done," Harper told the Brazilian. "Now you have your precious key, how about arranging a passport for me? I have a wife, a son, and a baby on the way. I'm not wandering around with you on a treasure hunt."

"But I still need your help, Harper."

"What's the matter? Can't you figure out how to place the key in a lock?"

"If only it were that simple. The bookcase is still in the former Presidential Palace, which is now a museum. Furthermore, the room in question is not open to the public. I need you to gain access."

"Have you lost the use of your legs, Federico? How about you go there yourself?"

"I might be recognized. You, a stranger, have a better chance of getting into Batista's office."

Karmina, having overheard the conversation, come out of the

kitchen. "As an amateur sleuth, Harper, I am sure you are good at sneaking around undetected."

The American lost heart to raising further objections. Remembering how Federico had helped him escape the prison and Karmina had driven them from the east end of the island, he decided to refuse was being unkind, and so he relented. "Okay, I'll help you, Federico, provided you keep your promise on the passport."

"Deal. Are you going to the museum right now?"

"After we've eaten lunch. You're buying, by the way," Harper confirmed. "And make sure you take us to a proper restaurant this time, one that has air conditioning as well as food."

Over their meal, Harper began giving some thought to his foray into the former Presidential suite. In the end, he decided it best if he went by himself. The Brazilian did not object, saying he needed to file a story with his syndicate. On the other hand, Karmina wanted to tag along. As a compromise, they agreed she could tour the rest of the museum, while Harper played at being a burglar.

21

THE PAIR WALKED PAST THE MUSEUM GUARD, OUT OF THE BUILDING, and down the steps. Harper stopped for a moment to link arms with Karmina.

"Well, did you find anything?"

"Not now, Karmina. I'll tell you later. Come on. This way."

Steering her south, he began hustling her along *Avenida de las Misiones*, at a brisk pace, in the opposite direction to where the car was parked.

"Stop; we are going the wrong way."

"Trust me. we're not," the American insisted. "And try to walk a little faster."

At the first opportunity, Harper hailed a taxi. As soon the vehicle stopped, he bundled Karmina into the rear passenger seat, jumped in next to her, and issued a curt directive to the cabbie, "Drive!"

Twenty minutes later, the pair were dropped off three blocks away from the apartment. During the ride, Harper kept looking out of the rear window and repeatedly shushing Karmina to be quiet.

As they started walking, the Cuban asked, "Why the cloak-and-dagger stuff, Harper? We tell *el taxista* [the cabbie] to take a circuitous route through the older part of the city, and we are still streets away from my place. What is going on?"

"As soon as we stepped outside the Presidential Palace, we picked up a tail," he told her. "Two men, to be precise, who took turns shadowing us."

Although he did not tell Karmina, having probed one man's mind, he had discovered that many of the thoughts inside his head were in German, which begged the question, *Why German?* Whatever the answer, he did not believe the man had their welfare as his primary concern.

Harper paused in his stride when he heard the sound of a siren in the distance. A few seconds later, a police car hurried past them despite the narrow street.

"Someone is in a rush," Harper observed. "I wonder what that is all about."

ABOUT TO CROSS *CALLE LUZ*, A SECOND POLICE CAR SCREAMED BY.

"Busy place," the American remarked. "I'll have you know, Karmina, that Cuba has one of the lowest crime rates in the world, but I'm sure you know that already."

"Quit stalling, Harper, and tell me how you managed to enter Batista's office."

"*No hay problema.* I just strolled up to the door and went in."

"Really?"

"After I succeeded in getting it unlocked, that is."

"You are a man of many talents. You can pick locks, I assume?" the young woman added, sarcastically

"Hardly, Karmina. I stood there, rattling the door handles until one of the curators approached. He addressed me in Spanish, of course, and I presumed he was asking how he might help. I replied, *He perdido la llave de mi habitación.*"

"I have lost my room key," she translated.

"Precisely. One of many must-know phrases I read in a Spanish phrasebook found on a shelf at your place. It's titled ONE THOUSAND AND ONE PHRASES A TOURIST SHOULD LEARN BEFORE VISITING SPAIN."

Karmina laughed. "That old thing. I bought it at a secondhand book market in *El Plaza de Armas*. I'm glad you were able to put it to good use."

"What's more," Harper continued, "if I get lost, I can ask for directions to the railway station, or, if I need to take a leak, to the nearest public toilet."

"And what if we need to get back to the apartment, *en seguida*, and not stand around chatting all day?"

"*En seguida*? I haven't a clue what you mean, Karmina. That phrase was not in the primer."

"Right now, Harper. At once. Straight away. Do you catch my drift?"

"Okay. Okay. You've made your point." The American put his arms up in mock surrender. "Come on; I believe we're nearly there."

They rounded the corner and stopped dead in their tracks. After a second's delay, Harper stepped back, pulling the Cuban with him, so they stayed out of sight.

"What is going on?" Karmina inquired.

"I don't know," Harper replied, "but there is an ambulance and two police cars parked in the square. Also, there's a crowd of onlookers. That can't be good."

She took a quick peek for herself. "A policeman is standing on the balcony of my apartment. Do you think Federico has had an accident? We should go see."

"Not a good idea," Harper replied.

"My thoughts, exactly." The words came from a man who was walking towards them. Dressed in the garb of a priest, he wore a full collar shirt and cassock. "*Señorita* y *señor*, you will be arrested if you do not follow me."

The priest's car was to be found further along the street, a safe distance from the apartment. A 1955 Chevrolet Bel Air, in pristine condition with its maroon bodywork and beige roof, the chrome gleamed as if it had just rolled off the North Tarrytown assembly line.

"Nice wheels," Harper remarked. "Once upon a time, cars like this were all the rage in my country."

"You must be referring to America, *señor* Harper." The priest smiled and held out his hand. "Don't worry. I am a friend of Federico. You may call me Father Marcolata. Hurry. Get in the car. I will explain along the way."

"Where are we going?" Harper asked as the priest took a roundabout route through the streets, regularly checking in his rearview mirror that they were not being followed.

"You'll see my friends. Fortunately, the two of you were not in the apartment when it was raided."

"The ambulance, was that for Federico?"

"I am afraid so," Father Marcolata replied. "I was ascending the stairs to the third floor when two men rushed past me. When I got to the apartment, the door was ajar, and I could see poor Federico laying prostrate on the floor."

"Is he dead?" Karmina asked, bluntly.

"Fortunately, no. Unconscious, yes. When the paramedics arrived, he had lapsed into a coma. I saw papers and books strewn across the floor, along with tossed cushions from the upturned couch."

The Chevrolet had reached *Avenida Rancho Boyeros*. They headed south towards the city outskirts.

"Those two men, who passed you, were obviously searching for something," Karmina decided.

"And they found what they were looking for, I believe," the priest informed them, regret in his voice. "One was carrying a wealth of documents. The other a computer and something else. I think it was a clock. Strange choice if they were stealing goods to sell. I should think it was hardly worth anything."

Harper realized Father Marcolata was referring to the carriage clock that had belonged to Esteban Ventura. Unsure how the priest fitted into all of this, or whether he could be trusted, the American stayed silent.

Karmina, having no such reservations, voiced her opinion. "I bet they were after Federico's notes. Did you happen to see if one of the men was carrying a book with a leather cover, Father?"

"As a matter of fact, I did. Good Lord. They have *capitán de policía* Ventura's journal. I wonder why they would take that?"

"Same reason they took the computer and documents. They wanted to find out what our journalist friend knows."

"Then they have everything," the priest said, despondently. "Now, we shall never solve the mystery."

"What mystery?" Harper asked, failing to see a connection.

23

FATHER MARCOLATA DROVE UNTIL THEY REACHED MAZORRA, NAMED after a colonial estate that occupied the area at one time. He turned off *Calle 275* into the courtyard of an old mission church and killed the car's engine. "Okay, *mis amigos*. This is where I live and work. You are welcome to stay as my guests until we can figure out what is going on."

Harper viewed the white stucco and exposed red brick that formed the front facade of *Iglesia de Nuestra Señora de la Merced* [Church of Our Lady of Mercy], as they walked towards the oak double doors.

Above loomed what would have been an imposing three-story bell tower that cried out for a stonemason to fix its crumbling engaged columns and cornices.

At variance with his crinkled face and snow-white hair, suggesting he was in his early seventies, with a youthful stride, Father Marcolata led the way. Pushing hard on the unlocked door, he entered. Inside, the air smelled of incense and candle wax. Two dozen pews lined the aisle on both sides, the majority covered in a thick layer of chalky dust. The altar was a simple affair, with its table covered in a plain white cloth and patternless frontal.

As the priest made his way toward the vestry, Father Marcolata took a moment to rehook a prayer cushion onto the back of a pew, allowing Harper time to approach a side table and pick up a pewter collection plate. "I thought Catholic churches were rich. Where are the gold candlesticks and chalices?"

"This is a poor man's church, in a sad state of disrepair," the priest, who retained the hearing of a bat, replied.

Taking a moment to gaze at the rough carving of Christ on The Cross, affixed to the wall behind the altar, Harper noted how well it fitted in with its meager surroundings. "Sad indeed," the American agreed.

The vestry, which served as the priest's office, was equally mundane. Drab-looking vestments hung on a hook by the door. Karmina walked over and fingered one of the threadbare garments and muttered, *Triste de hecho*; the same remark, in Spanish, made by Harper a minute earlier.

A desk, set by the window, was littered with papers. Father Marcolata busied himself sifting through the untidiness, searching for something.

"Ah; here it is," the priest declared, pulling out a document from under the papers. It was a newspaper clipping.

The American took a cursory glance. Seeing it was in Spanish, he handed it back to Father Marcolata, who translated the report of thirty people from various parts of the island disappearing. All occurred within ten days, during the night, both men and women between eighteen and thirty years of age. The article was dated two years ago, almost to the day.

"Don't you see?" the priest continued enthusiastically, "It's all linked."

"To what?" Harper asked.

"To Esteban Ventura's journal," Father Marcolata replied. "The Police *Captán* refers to patients from the asylum going missing as well, although that was some twenty years earlier."

Harper questioned the assertion, saying, "That's a bit of a stretch, with such a time gap, surely?"

"In both instances, I am convinced these people were all taken for the same reason," the priest persisted.

"Which is?" Harper held his breath, awaiting enlightenment.

"Scientific experiments. And I would stake my reputation on the perpetrator being Doctor Carlos Fuentes, former Director of the now-closed Psychiatric Hospital across the street from this very building."

Harper sat on the corner of the desk and scratched the back of his head. "Father, none of this adds up. Federico told me about Fuentes fleeing the country in '57, avoiding arrest by the Authorities following abuses, even deaths, of some of his patients. Captain Ventura wrote a note in his journal that he believed Batista tipped the Doctor off. Apparently, they were close friends. And now you're saying the fact that people went missing a couple of years ago is somehow connected. If you're are right, that would imply Fuentes came back to Cuba. I find that hard to believe."

"Think what you may, señor Harper. I am going to make some coffee. Would you and Karmina like a cup?"

The priest walks over to a hotplate in the corner, placed a kettle on the ring, and turned it on. While he waited for the water to boil, he gave the American a quick tutorial on the worldwide network of clerics that funneled answers to any question one chose to put out there. In this case, the previous whereabouts of señor Carlos Fuentes.

"Having left Cuba in a hurry, the Doctor's first port of call was Argentina, where he teams up with none other than the Nazi war criminal Josef Mengele in the city of Olivos. What the pair of them did there is unknown. Fuentes only stayed a few weeks. He then flew to the United States, with a stopover in Paraguay for a few days, meeting with an international banker."

Harper and Karmina listen without interrupting, as Father Marcolata continued, "Fuentes spent time in Boston, Philadelphia, and Houston. The very same cities that house the Harvard, Perelman, and Baylor Medical Schools, by the way. Eventually, he settles down in Columbus, Georgia, where he changes his name to …" The shriek of the kettle's whistle began, announcing the water was boiling. It crescendoed as he spoke the last few words, leaving Harper to deduce what had been said; *hide his old identity*.

Father Marcolata stood up, went to the cupboard under the hotplate, and removed three mugs and a tin of *Cubita* instant coffee.

Columbus. Harper knew the city well, being a short drive from Fort Benning, where he was stationed during his military service.

A few minutes later the priest returned, holding cups of steaming black coffee, and resumed his narrative.

"Fuentes practices general medicine, marries a woman much younger than himself, and raises a family. The good Doctor became a pillar of the community, well respected, elected to the Board of the local hospital. And then, suddenly, out of the blue, in 1978 he ups and leaves, returning to Cuba."

"All this from your network of spies?" Harper skeptically asked.

"I would not use the word *spies*, exactly," the Father Marcolata objected. "More like well-meaning informants. Who are highly reliable, I might add."

"Okay. Assuming what you say is correct, two questions: Why did Carlos Fuentes come back, and where precisely is he now?"

"I don't know why," the priest replied with a glum face. "What I can tell you is, a year after his return, he dies."

"From what?" Harper inquired.

"Old age, presumably, He would have been in his late seventies. There was never an autopsy, and the body was cremated, so we shall never know."

"Cremation? Isn't that rather unconventional in this part of the world?" Karmina commented.

"Not if you are trying to cover something up," Harper argued. "However, I believe it is of little relevance. If Fuentes is long dead, how can he be linked to people gone missing more recently?"

"I can assure you, *señor* Harper, he is." Father Marcolata responded. "During Confession, people reveal to their priest things they will never admit to their husbands, wives, or best friends."

24

As the three of them sat in the vestry drinking more coffee, Father Marcolata continued talking about the abducted men and women. He told of others going missing from time to time. Superstitious locals suspected a mythical ghost-monster was spiriting them away. The priest was having none of this and reiterated they were being abducted for experimentation.

Harper offered more logical explanations, suggesting the missing persons may have died far from home without identification or left of their own free will to live somewhere else and take advantage of better employment.

"You mentioned earlier the psychiatric hospital. When was it closed?" Karmina asked.

"Shortly after the Revolution. There was an inquiry after the allegations against Fuentes and the other doctors. Despite changes to the staff and imposition of outside supervision, in general, the patients continued to be treated poorly. When Castro came to power, as part of his health care reform, he ordered the place closed for good. In the morning, you and your American friend should take a look for yourself, although I should warn you it's a depressing place. It reminds me of how badly some people mistreat others, especially in this case, under the pretext of making them well."

Later, Father Marcolata escorted Harper and Karmina to the presbytery, a building detached from the church that was his living quarters. A modest dwelling, somewhat in character with the church itself, the couple were shown separate bedrooms. From time to time, the priest explained, he allowed homeless or displaced persons to use his home as temporary accommodation.

Before retiring for the night, they ate a simple supper of goat's cheese, bread, and fresh fruit.

Karmina started expressing her concern over Federico's well being. The American assured her that the hospital was the best place her boyfriend could be right now, while Father Marcolata said he would offer up prayers for a speedy recovery.

"But is he safe?" she asked. "Are any of us safe? Who knows, we could be attacked at any moment."

"For what reason, my child?" the priest responded. "I believe whoever went to your apartment was their solely to take the computer and journal. Poor Federico got in the way, that is all."

"But his research papers, he has kept at my place forever. Why would those thugs go their now?"

"Something tipped their hand," Harper suggested. "As we left the Museum today, we were followed. Maybe that was the trigger." The American took his last bite of cheese and stood up. "I don't believe there is any point in speculating. Now, if you'll both excuse me, I'm going to get some sleep. See you both in the morning."

With that, Harper retired for the night, leaving Karmina still brooding, and Father Marcolata trying to reassure her.

Once in bed, the American could not sleep. His subconscious was telling him the stories about the missing individuals were important, but he could not figure out how. With effort, he steered his mind to more pleasant thoughts of Julia, Oliver, and the baby. *The baby? What is its name? Jules and I never got around to choosing one before I left.*

Harper started compiling a list. Alice. Beatrice. Charlotte. Diane. Edwina. Felicity. Harper never got past 'F'; he had drifted off to sleep.

With a sudden jerk, the American was wide awake. The clock on the nightstand showed 3:25. He turned over but could not fall back to sleep. A phrase Father Marcolata had said resurfaced in his conscious mind. H*ide his old identity.* Hide, as in conceal, or Hyde, as in the name? If the latter, then Fuentes' had changed his name to Hyde. Moreover, *Hyde* was one of the two doctors who succeeded in altering my brain patterns producing my mind-reading abilities.

The American lay there, in is head doing the math. *Assuming Fuentes, aka Hyde, was a friend of General Batista, they were probably about the same age, which made him too old to be my attending physician.* He let the thought marinate. *However, not if said doctor was Fuentes' son, assuming at least one child was a boy.*

Harper had established a tenuous link, providing him with a new incentive to help both the priest and the reporter.

Reporter. As that word popped into his mind, the American wondered how Federico was doing, deciding he should visit him, but not before he had inspected the asylum that so excited Father Marcolata. "What secrets does the place hold?" Harper asked himself. "One way or another I'll find out, and then there will be a story to share with you, *mi viejo amigo* [my old friend]. We'll have that boo*k* of yours written yet."

25

IN THE DISTANCE, HARPER COULD SEE A YOUNG BOY WAVING AT HIM. In some way, the child seemed familiar. The American pushed through the crush of people, at times losing sight of the small figure, only to see him again a few moments later.

The boy would stop from time to time, allowing Harper to get nearer, and then scamper off as though he were playing a game of hide-and-seek. However, if this was a game, the American was not enjoying it.

Harper pressed on, weaving through the flotilla of swimming pools, water slides and spray jets.

I'm not playing this silly game, he told himself, having stopped to catch his breath. *I am going back to find Oliver and Julia. Then I'm going to buy ice-cream and sit in the shade.*

The boy shouted from halfway up the stairs leading to the top of a giant waterslide

Olly? Was that Oliver's voice?

Breaking into a trot, Harper nudged people aside. He reached the bottom and looked skyward. The giant structure was remarkably similar to one in the *Atlantis Marine and Waterpark,* just a short distance from their luxury beachfront villa in Palm Jumeirah, Dubai.

The boy was already at the uppermost platform, leaning over the railings, waving.

———

"You made it," the boy said by way of greeting, as Harper competed the climb. "Why were you away from home for so long?"

"Away? I haven't been anywhere."

"Mom says otherwise. She misses you. I do too."

The boy flung his arms around Harper's thighs. *Funny*, the American thought to himself, *I don't recall Olly being so short. Or so young for that matter.* "Wait a second. You're not Oliver."

"Who says I am?"

"How old are you, son?" Harper asked.

"Old enough to go down the giant waterslide on my own," was the reply.

"No, you're not. Where are your parents?" The young lad shrugged his shoulders. "In that case, I'm coming with you."

———

The pair settled onto the rubber raft that would take them down the slide, aided by the jets of water that provided the lubrication beneath them. With one arm around the boy, Harper pushed away with the other. They began to gather speed, going faster as the chute became steeper.

"Woooow," Harper exclaimed involuntarily as the descent became a vertical drop. The lad and the raft were plummeting below him, while he seemed to tumble in slow motion.

"No," Harper cried as he hit the water, sending up a geyser of spray. Splashing frantically, it took him a moment to resurface. "Where are you, son?" he screamed. in panic.

There was no reply, only the raft bobbing gently on the water.

"WAKE UP, HARPER. YOU WERE HAVING A BAD DREAM," FATHER
Marcolata told the American as he vigorously shook his shoulder.
"Are you all right?"

"I dreamt a small boy had drowned. We went down a slide at a
water park in Dubai, and the lad disappeared." Harper pressed his
hand against his forehead, trying to push the image from his mind.

"You are not at any waterpark; you are here in Cuba."

"Yes, Cuba," Harper responded, rubbing his eyes. "I remember
now."

"Here. Take a drink of water, amigo, and you will feel better."

"Thank you, Father." The American took a sip. "What time
is it?"

"Almost six o'clock. It's too early to eat."

"I'm sorry if I woke you," Harper apologized.

The priest laughed. "I am usually up at this hour. God never
sleeps. I needed to get ready for this morning's mass."

"Do you get many communicants?" the American asked,
remembering seeing dust covering most of the pews.

"A handful at best; sometimes none. Why don't you try to go
back to sleep."

"I think I'll take a walk if it's all the same to you. I need to get some fresh air and clear my head. I'll see you shortly."

A cool breeze blew against Harper's face as he left the presbytery. Crickets were to be heard chirping in the grounds of the abandoned hospital. Looking in that direction, the American thought he saw movement in the shadows. A ghost of a fertile imagination, or was somebody watching? Harper, only half awake, was disinclined to check. Instead, the American rounded the corner of the church and sat on the entrance steps. He buried his face in his hands, taking deep breaths, trying to calm down. But calm down, he could not. He had had weird dreams in the past, often setting a prelude to something terrible about to happen. These forebodings, in general, were obscure, only decipherable after the fact. Harper racked his brain, trying to figure out what the image of the drowned boy meant.

His thoughts were interrupted by the voice of Father Marcolata. "Are you sure you are all right, *señor* Harper?"

"I thought you had a communion to give, Father. Don't worry about me. I'll be fine, out here, on my own."

The sun broke over the horizon.

"I was checking on you before starting Mass. You shouldn't be out here by yourself. Why don't you join me inside the church?"

"Okay, I will." Harper got to his feet.

The priest placed a hand on the American's shoulder. With a smile, he said, "In that case, I will be assured of a congregation of least one this morning."

AFTER BREAKFAST, HARPER VENTURED ACROSS THE STREET, PICKING his way through blocks of fallen masonry and patches of undergrowth, until he reached the steps of what was originally a colonial mansion with add-ons as the mental hospital had expanded. Karmina was close on his heels.

The front door hung askew, partly blocking their way in. After squeezing through the gap, they found a large hallway. From there the pair began exploring the ground floor. That found a reception room, with peeling wallpaper, which contained a couch, the rotting leather covering exposing a termite-infested wooden frame. Next door, a dining area presented nothing but broken chairs and smashed china. The commercial kitchen had been stripped of its stoves, sinks, preparation tables, and ancillary equipment. To the right of the main entrance was a waiting room, with an adjacent consulting room. A desk remained in one, a medicine cabinet in the other. Everything else of value had been removed, probably looted, Harper concluded.

From the hallway, a grandiose staircase curved up to the second floor. The couple stepped carefully, as some of the stair-treads suffered from wet rot. The same soft, spongy timber was to be found on the landing and in the wards. In one wing, they found small rooms, stereotyped padded cells, the hallmark of a lunatic asylum. One, in particular, caught the American's attention. On the walls was an abundance of graffiti. In white chalk, the phrase **Te Amo** stood out. In capitals, below and to the left, was another; UN MUNDO DE BIEN. Karmina translated, *I love you* and *a world of good.* However, scribbled diagonally across the two was the single word, REBELIÓN, written in bright-red lettering. *Whoever the writer, full marks for coming up with the paint,* Harper decided. "What's the connection between the three phrases, Karmina?" he asked.

"I suspect they were written by different patients, so most likely there isn't one," the Cuban suggested. "Who knows what went on inside the minds of those poor tortured souls. May they now rest in peace."

"Amen to that," the American replied, deciding he had seen enough. Harper suggested they return to the entrance vestibule. Once there, he noticed another, less ornate, set of stairs that descended to the basement. However, as soon as the stairwell turned back on itself, rubble, which almost reached the ceiling, blocked their path.

With no hope of climbing over, Harper decided to call it a day and proposed they return to the presbytery.

The priest was nowhere in sight.

"I'll go look for Father Marcolata," Harper volunteered, "and inform him the way to the basement is blocked. Are you coming with me, Karmina?"

"No, not right now. I still haven't got over the shock of what happened yesterday. I think I'll lie down for a while if it's all the same to you?"

"Sure. I understand. Get some rest."

Trying to push the oppressiveness of the mental hospital to the back of his mind, the American set off towards the church.

Father Marcolata was not inside the church itself, nor the vestry. Eventually, Harper found the priest, dressed in a stain covered beige boiler suit, applying mortar to a part of the exterior wall where the stucco had broken away.

"You're a jack-of-all-trades, I see. Do you want me to lend a hand? If you like, I can mix more cement."

"Thank you, Harper, but no. I have almost finished here, and the other part of the wall that needs attention is presently in full sunlight. I have learned from experience it's a fool's errand to render hot stonework. If you do, it will crack within a few weeks." The priest paused from his labor and asked, "Did you find anything of interest in the asylum?"

"Only abandonment and decay. The place had a strange smell, and I'm not talking about the wet rot or the profusion of mold."

"I know what you mean. If you asked me, it had the smell of death."

"I couldn't get to the basement. There had been a cave-in of sorts. Do you know anything about that, Father?"

"Indeed, I do. About ten years ago, if I remember correctly, explosives were used to collapse of the ceiling."

"But why?"

"To keep people out, of course." Then the priest smiled. "But not *all* people. Give me a few minutes, and I'll show you another way in."

FATHER MARCOLATA RETRIEVED A RING OF KEYS THAT WERE hanging on a hook next to his vestments. He then made his way towards the church entrance. Harper followed.

Inside the place of worship, immediately to the left, was an arched door, recessed into the stonework. Once unlocked, the American observed it was the way up to the bell tower, via a rickety vertical ladder. However, the priest directed him to a steep set of steps, carved into the *Gtünes* limestone, providing means of entry to what Harper presumed would be the crypt.

He was wrong. In the dim light of a lantern, the American perceived a wrought iron gate blocking access to a tunnel running north. Selecting another key, the priest unlocked the barrier. With a creak of rusting hinges, he pushed it inwards.

"This will take you to the basement of the hospital," Father Marcolata explained, as he unclipped another key from the keyring. "At the far end, you will find a steel-plated door. This key will unlock it. Good luck."

"Aren't you coming with me, Father?"

"You're a big boy, Harper. You don't need me to hold your

hand. I'm going back to repointing some of the church's masonry. See you shortly."

After handing over the lantern, the priest did an about-face and re-climbed the steps.

The American felt a shiver go down his back. "Why does this place give me the willies?" he asked himself out loud.

Receiving no answer, Harper set off, keeping his head low, accompanied by any demons his mind chose to conjure up.

HARPER UNLOCKED THE STEEL DOOR, PULLING IT OPEN, HE ventured inside. To his left was a passage leading to the collapsed stairwell. Directly in front of him was the doorless entrance to a large room, its walls characterized by flaking paint and patches of pervasive black mold. In rows on either side were a dozen or more porcelain-enameled cast iron bathtubs. Rust stained, a thick brown dried-out sludge lined their bottoms. The corroded taps looked as though they had not been turned on in decades. At the opposite end of every bathtub was a four-foot-tall metal box. Facing outward were sets of dials and meters. Coils of electric wiring snaked from outlets, terminating in what remained of leather skullcaps, each studded with round flat copper electrodes.

The American shuddered as he imaged a patient being subjected to a bath of ice-cold water, electricity flowing through their brain, all the stuff of a mad scientist movie.

Moving on, at the end of the right-hand passage was a second steel door. Harper prayed it would not be locked. He was in luck. This room was the epitome of a chemistry lab, except the benches were strewn with the broken glass from retorts and flasks. More of the same covered the floor, together with discolored sheets of paper and the occasional water-soaked notebook.

Someone made a mess during their hasty retreat, Harper decided, as he viewed the disorder that had overtaken the room.

He stopped and picked up one of the notebooks. Full of chemical formula, the handwriting was a lazy, almost indecipherable scrawl. Written in German to boot, Harper concluded there was little point in taking it as a memento of his visit.

The American spent two or three minutes surveying the place, before deciding to leave. He swung the lantern around as he turned towards the exit. Light reflected off the tempered safety glass that was a fume cabinet. Still intact, he wandered over and looked inside.

A pile of ash and fragments of scorched paper presented themselves, where someone had chosen to have a small bonfire. Harper lifted the hood and gently sifted through the larger pieces, finding some of the text still legible, but nothing meaningful. Notwithstanding, tucked in the far corner was a screwed-up sheet of paper, almost hidden by a tangle of cobwebs. Once flattened out, it revealed a hand-drawn schematic of a drug's chemical structure. Incomprehensible to Harper's non-scientific mind, his frustration was further compounded by the unfamiliar word **NOOTROP**, written in capitals, below the diagram. Nonetheless, Harper carefully refolded the sheet and placed it inside his jacket pocket, in case if it might be of some significance.

There was a crashing sound coming from the corridor. Then another as someone banged into a table or chair.

Harper heard a woman cursing in Spanish. "Karmina, is that you?" he called out.

A smiling face appeared in the doorway. "Who else would it be, Harper? Were you expecting *El Coco*?"

"*El Coco*; who is he?" the American asked.

"*El Coco*; *él es* the bogeyman."

30

For the second morning in a row, Harper attended Communion. Once over, the American followed Father Marcolata into the vestry.

While the priest was removing his vestments, he asked Harper, "Something is bothering you, my son. I can tell by the gaunt expression on your face. Is there something you care to share?"

The American nodded slowly and sat on the chair in front of the priest's desk. He waited until Marcolata sat down and began, "I have this gut feeling that something bad is going to happen. I don't know what exactly, or when, but it's most likely going to be worse than our reporter friend, Federico, getting a bang on the head."

The priest smiled. "If you mean here in the church, *señor* Harper, that is highly improbable. There is nothing worth stealing. I don't know how I can reassure you, except to tell you to have a little faith."

Harper hunched his shoulders, unconvinced. He sat for a moment thinking and then said, "I wonder if you'd do something for me?"

"Of course," the priest replied. "Ask away."

The American reached into his jacket pocket and removed the

creased paper containing the handwritten formula. Then he fumbled in his trouser pocket and produced the key that opened the drawer in former President Batista's office, together with a silver coin. He handed them over to Father Marcolata.

"You say the church is safe. Would you keep these things for me, until I can figure out what is going on?"

The priest took the items, placed them on his desk, and examined each in turn.

"This formula, is it important?"

"I have no idea," Harper replied. "I found it the asylum's laboratory. Hold on to it please, until I can find someone I can trust, who can tell what drug the diagram depicts."

"I can do that," Father Marcolata agreed. "And this would be the key mentioned in *Captán* Ventura's journal, I presume?"

"That's right. And the coin I found inside one of Batista's bookcase drawers at the Museum of the Revolution."

"Interesting," the priest remarked after turning the coin over. "This was minted to mark the fiftieth year of the Republic. Do you realize the other significance of the date on the back?"

Harper shook his head.

"1952 was the year Batista, with the army's backing, staged a coup and seized power." The priest turned the coins over once more, and added as an afterthought, "Perhaps it is all a coincidence. but I wonder why someone would bother to keep this particular minting in a locked drawer?"

"I have no idea, Father. Even as a collector's item, I assume it isn't particularly valuable."

The priest grunted, only half listening. He picked up the key and, with a snap, pressed the coin into the center of the circular indentation that was part of the key's shaft.

"A perfect fit," Father Marcolata remarked, "as if they were meant to complement each other. I'll put them where no one will think to look."

"How will *I* find them," the American inquired.

"You ask me, of course. Coming from you, Harper, that's a silly question. Now, unless you have anything more to say, I suggest we go back to the presbytery and find out what Karmina has prepared us for breakfast."

"Pancakes with maple syrup, maybe?"

"Don't get your hopes up. We are in Havana; not in New York City," the priest reminded him, with a chuckle. " If you're lucky, you will probably be served sliced bread, soaked in olive oil."

FATHER MARCOLATA HAD RECENTLY VISITED THE HOSPITAL WHERE Federico was recovering. After being told he was well enough to receive more visitors, Harper and Karmina elected to pay the reporter a social call.

Harper stalled the Chevrolet Bel Air three times in succession. Losing patience, Karmina demanded she should take over. They drove north for nine miles before turning right into *Avenida Salvador Allende*. After making a left turn at *Padre Verela*, it was a trouble-free drive to *Hospital Hermanos Ameijeiras*. The whole journey had taken less than forty minutes.

Having parked the car, it was a short walk to the foyer of the twenty-five-story building. From a booth adjacent to the hospital's gift shop, Karmina took the opportunity to purchase a bunch of flowers, and Harper a basket of fresh fruit. Then, after checking with the reception desk, they found Federico in a small sideward on the twelfth floor. He was sitting up in bed, watching television.

Once he had exchanged hugs and kisses with his girlfriend, the journalist's first words to the American were, by way of greeting. "Fruit and flowers, Harper; how thoughtful of you."

"The flowers are from Karmina; the fruit is from me. I wouldn't want people to get the wrong idea."

"And what idea is that, amigo? Your ugly face is no match for Karmina's beauty."

Considering he had suffered a severe concussion, the Brazilian seemed in good spirits.

"Do you know your computer was stolen from the apartment?" Harper inquired, ignoring the jibe.

"Yes, Father Marcolata told me. The journal as well, I gather. But it's not the end of the world."

"The priest thinks differently. Now that all your research is lost, Father Marcolata is concerned that he will never solve the mystery of the abductions. Whatever that's all about?"

"Time for explanations later. Pass me an orange, please."

"How can you be so cheerful, Federico?" the American asked.

The Brazilian laughed. "I thought you were a man of the world, Harper. Have you never heard of *electronic backups*? And what isn't in *the Cloud is* stored up here," he confided, tapping the side of his skull. "You should try some of this fruit," the reporter continued, his mouth full of food. "It is rather tasty."

Harper was not listening to Federico's banter. Instead he was watching the doorway, concerned that somebody with ill intent might have seen them enter the hospital.

"Cheer up, Harper," chimed Federico, trying to catch his attention. "Loose the glum face. This is not a funeral you're attending, you know. The doctors say I shall be well enough to go home in a few days."

"Not to the apartment, you won't. It's not safe," the American cautioned.

"Where then?"

"To Father Marcolata's place in *Mazorra*," Harper replied. "There, we can keep an eye on you."

"And who is going to keep an eye on *you*?" The Brazilian laughed once again as if this was one big joke. "*Deus no céu* [God in heaven]! Would you look at that, Harper? You're on the television."

Karmina and the American turned to face the screen. Although the news anchor was speaking Spanish, a photograph of Harper was displayed in the background.

"What's he saying?" Harper inquired, fearing their escape from GITMO had finally leaked.

"That you're a hero, dear boy. Sorry to say a dead hero, but a hero nonetheless. They are saying, you rushed into a burning cell block and released trapped prisoners. Unfortunately, you were overcome by smoke and died from severe burns."

"Really," the American scoffed. "Someone has a fertile imagination. It's an obvious cover-up. Nobody wants to broadcast that two prisoners escaped."

The Brazilian smiled and raised an eyebrow. "You know how it is, Harper? Journalists deal in many versions of the truth."

3 2

VISITING TIME OVER, HARPER AND KARMINA MADE THEIR WAY along the corridor. The American kept his head down, avoiding the security cameras. As they descended in the elevator, he worried he might be recognized, and someone would turn him in.

Nobody bothered to give him a second glance, the snippet of foreign news ignored as the locals got on with their daily lives.

They reached the foyer, the elevator doors opened, and the pair stepped out.

"Hold on, Karmina. I you to need to speak to someone at the desk."

After finding out the nearest public access point to the Internet, they walked towards the exit, Harper suggested they leave the Chevrolet in the parking lot for the time being and continue on foot.

A short stroll brought them to a snack café on the *Calle Javalar*. Once Harper had pulled up a browser, he began a search.

"What are you looking for?" Karmina asked.

"Not what; who. I'm supposed to be dead, and I want to find out what happened to my corpse."

> The deceased's ashes were delivered to next
> of kin.

That was the last thing Harper wanted to read about himself on the US newsfeeds, but there was little he could do about it unless he broke cover and contacted Julia directly.

Assuming I can find Aunt Cordelia's number. Harper mulled over whether or not that was a good idea, wondering if someone might be tapping the Savannah phone line. *Prudent to steer clear for the time being*, he decided, taking a moment to erase the browser's cache.

As soon as Karmina finished her coffee, the couple left the café and set off for the hospital's parking lot.

Harper continued the internal conversation with himself. *Even if Jules doesn't accept that I am dead, without a passport, and the airports and harbors watched, I have no way of leaving the island.*

His concern was not just the Authorities but the men who had ransacked Karmina's apartment. *Who are these bad guys, anyway? All I know is one speaks German.*

Harper remembered Father Marcolata telling him Carlos Fuentes, having left Cuba, journeyed to Argentina and stayed for a short while at a German-speaking enclave. He decided, somehow, this was connected with Hyde.

In his mind, Harper circled back to the priest's comment that Hyde's father had returned to Cuba before his death. *Is that where Hyde Junior is right now?*

The American paused in his stride. Something was still bothering him concerning Hyde Junior. He stood for a moment, allowing the thought to surface into his consciousness. *Hyde Junior is dead! He died when I used telekinesis to force him into the clock mechanism, in the tower high above the Houses of Parliament. So who is really behind it all?*

With a spring in his last few steps, the American decided it was time to find out by remarking, "Once more, the game is afoot."

"*¿Qué*, Harper? You're making no sense. What game?" Karmina shook her head, concluding her companion was just another crazy American.

Walking through the parking lot, they reached the priest's Chevrolet.

"You can drive, Karmina," Harper suggested, handing over the key. "We need to get back to the church."

A couple of minutes later, as the Bel Air reached the main road, Harper glanced to the rear. Once satisfied nobody was following, he leaned back in his seat and relaxed.

Five minutes passed.

"What's going on, Harper? Aren't you going to tell me?"

"It's quite simple, my dear Watson. When you have eliminated the impossible, whatever remains, however improbable, must be the truth. I need to speak with Father Marcolata again. I believe he, and he alone, knows the truth."

33

As soon as the Chevrolet drew into the forecourt of the church, they could tell something was amiss. At the foot of the steps, the wheelbarrow the priest had been using lay on its side. Tools were scattered on the ground. There were scuff marks in the gravel indicating a possible struggle.

Harper hurried inside the church proper and found the pews no longer in orderly rows. Prayer cushions were slashed, and the hog hair filling scattered about. The altar cloth was askew. On the floor lay a candle, crushed into small pieces by a heavy boot. The baptismal font had been toppled off its pedestal. No mean feat considering its weight. Even the cross had been ripped off the wall.

The priest was nowhere to be seen.

"Maybe Father Marcolata has been kidnapped?" Karmina suggested.

"Maybe. But why wreck the place in the process. It is not as though the good Father is a man of heavy build. I wouldn't expect him to put up much of a struggle. Let's keep looking."

The American walked over to the ached recess and tried the door that gave access to the bell tower and the basement. It was locked.

Meanwhile, Karmina had made her way to the vestry. As she opened the door, a metallic, slightly sweet odor assaulted her nostrils. It was coming from the shadowed area in the far corner of the room.

Taking a few steps nearer, seeing more clearly, she stopped dead in her tracks and screamed.

The American resisted the need to retch as bile rose from his stomach. The priest lay on his side, blood still oozing from his stomach. Harper did not need his experience serving in the military to know the man had been stabbed.

Close to tears, Karmina asked, "His he dead?"

"I am afraid so," Harper replied.

Quickly the American made his way to the coat hooks near the door and removed the nearest vestment. Returning, he closed Father Marcolata's eyes, before covering the body. Only then did he read the blood-smeared handwriting on the wall.

Mateo 22:20-21

"It's from the bible," Harper declared, stating the obvious. "Hold on a second. I'll find the verses."

All the bibles had been swept off the bookshelf onto the floor. Harper picked up the one closest to him. Written in Spanish, of course, he handed the scripture to Karmina. She took only a few seconds to turn to the right page, and read the verses aloud:

"*20* Entonces les dice: ¿De quién es esta imagen, y lo que está encima escrito?

21 Ellos le dicen: De César. Y les dijo: Pagad pues a César lo que es de César, y a Dios lo que es de Dios."

"What's the translation?" Harper asked.

"Then he tells them: Whose image is this, and what is written above?

They say: Of César. And he said to them: Pay then to Caesar what belongs to Caesar, and to God what belongs to God."

The American repeated the words, "Pay then to Caesar what belongs to Caesar, and to God what belongs to God. Is this a message, left by the Father, for us? If so, what does it mean?"

Karmina, who had seated herself on the couch, did not answer. Face in her hands; she was openly sobbing.

Resisting the urge to comfort her, the American tentatively lifted the corner of the vestment and took a closer look at the body. The priest had bled out as a result of receiving numerous stab wounds, not deep enough to kill immediately but severe enough to inflict pain. Father Marcolata had been tortured.

"Were they looking for the key, coin, and formula I had entrusted to you, Father? Did you give up any information?" Harper asked the corpse. "Clearly not, otherwise the perpetrators would not have turned over this room and the church. I expect, they tossed the presbytery as well; am I right?"

The dead priest did not reply.

"It's best we leave, Karmina," Harper decided. "Let me help you up."

His arm around the young woman's shoulders, offering words of comfort, the American led her from the room. Back in the church proper, Harper looked about, repeating to himself, *Pay then to Caesar what belongs to Caesar, and to God what belongs to God*, still at a loss to what the priest was trying to convey.

3 4

"Sit down for a few minutes, Karmina. I want to take another look round."

"If it were me, where would I hide a key?" the American muttered to himself.

There were not many places that had not been investigated by the intruders. Harper lifted the apron and looked under the altar. He found only fragments of a stale wafer, dropped during the Eucharist.

The floor was made up of stone pavers. Nothing presented itself that one had been lifted recently.

He walked over to the cross. The outstretched arms of Christ had snapped on both sides. Shards of the crown of thorns lay on the ground, broken off by the fall. Someone had turned the crucifix over. Harper could see the marks of a knifepoint that had been used to check if the carving was hollow inside.

Harper crouched down, taking his time to examine the underside of each bench, but found no key affixed.

Standing up again, the American swiveled himself around on the balls of his feet.

"There's nothing here!" Harper exclaimed in frustration.

"Come on, Father; what were you trying to tell me? What things are Caesar's?"

Money!

The revelation was like a blinding light.

"Where would the church keep its money? Does it even have any money?"

"Try the offering box." It was Karmina who spoke. She had roused herself and was now standing behind Harper. As the American turned around, she continued, "I noticed it by the front door when we came in."

Sure enough, just inside the entrance was a wooden box attached to the wall. It had a slot in the top for donations.

"Karmina, you're a genius," Harper pronounced as he tried lifting the lid. "It's locked. I should go and see if I can find the key in the vestry."

The young woman smiled, stepping aside as he made his way down the center aisle.

There was a sound of splintering wood. Harper stopped, turned, and walked back. Karmina was holding a hymnal in her right hand, its spine damaged.

"I guess there's no need to bother after all," Harper concluded. Bending down, he picked up the key with its coin insert, together with the folded paper, which was the formula. "I've found what I'm looking for."

Harper decided he owed it to Father Marcolata to inform the police.

Not until we are well clear of this place, he told himself. *The last thing we need is to become suspects in a murder inquiry. And maybe Karmina should be the one making the phone call. I don't want to draw attention to my American accent.*

We can use the priest's car. Stealing another one isn't the smart move.

Before leaving, Harper checked the trunk and found a wheel jack, lug wrench, a pair of jumper cables, and a screwdriver. He had an idea.

Putting the last item into his jacket pocket, he slammed the lid, walked to where his companion was standing, and pointed to the driver's seat. His chauffeur climbed in and patiently waited for the American to do the same.

"Where to, boss?" Karmina asked, with a sweet smile.

"North, towards Havana. I'm sure we'll come across a couple of unattended cars or trucks along the way. We need to *borrow* their number plates."

They were two miles from the church when Harper spotted signage for Habana Golf Club. "Turn here," he told Karmina, pointing. She slowed and turned right.

Reaching the parking lot, they chose a secluded spot away from the clubhouse. Karmina did as instructed and turned off the ignition. Harper exited the vehicle, screwdriver in hand, and proceeded towards the nearest car.

It took five minutes to remove the number plates from the priest's car and two others. The American put Father Marcolata's plates on the first vehicle, the first vehicle's plates on the second vehicle, and the second vehicle's plates on the Chevrolet.

"That should keep them guessing for a while. The owners probably won't notice the switch," Harper announced, with satisfaction. Once the American had climbed back into the Bel Air, the young woman backtracked until they were again on *Avenida Rancho Boyeros*.

"Where are we going to stay?" Karmina asked. "A hotel?"

"Not a hotel. They'll ask me for a passport, which I don't have. Since we can no longer take Federico to the presbytery, our best options to use your apartment. We can even try to straighten the place up a bit before he gets out of the hospital."

"But you told Federico the place was not safe," Karmina reminded the American.

"We'll just have to take our chances," Harper replied, "unless you've got a better idea."

"Not really. Besides, it will be nice to sleep in my bed again."

"And I can get used to the couch, once more," Harper added, trying to make light of a bad situation. "Stop somewhere on the way to make that phone call, and I'll buy something to eat and a pack of beer."

It was another eight miles before they reached the *Boyeros y Camaguey* shopping mall. While Harper purchased some provisions, Karmina placed a phone call to the police. Then they headed for Old Havana.

The apartment was in total disarray. Worse than the church, it looked as though whoever had done this threw furniture around to make a point. Harper and Karmina ate an early dinner before going to bed. The cleanup could wait until morning.

For the American, sleep did not come easily, wondering why the key and paper containing the formula were so crucial. *Where they the same men who took Federico's computer and Captain Ventura's journal?*

Harper stared at the ceiling, his eyes tracing the shadow patterns produced by the partly closed slatted shutters. None provided a pathway to enlightenment. One thing for sure, keeping the key, coin, and formula in his possession, was asking for more trouble. To that end, he continued to lie there, wide-awake, until he came up with a plan to place the items somewhere out of harm's way.

THE NEXT MORNING, HARPER SUGGESTED TO KARMINA SHE straighten the apartment.

"Stop treating me like your personal maid," she protested, huffily. "You can help as well. or is that beneath your dignity?"

"I have an errand to run, and I don't need a chaperone."

"I don't see why I should do all work on my own. Take me with you," Karmina demanded.

"No," the American adamantly replied.

"Admit it, Harper, you're a hopeless driver, and you need me to keep you out of trouble. I'll buy you breakfast."

At the thought of eating something more substantial than bread and cheese, the American backed down. He was proposing to contact a person who resided on the western seaboard of the United States. In the Pacific Time Zone, it would only be 5:00 in the morning. However, the American needed to locate him first.

Leaving the apartment, once they reached *Murillia*, which changed to *Dragones,* it was another mile to the intersection of *Amistad.* Continuing a further sixty yards, Harper found what he was looking for on his right; a café with Internet access.

It took the American thirty minutes before he had an actual

location for Seong-ho Moon, an immigrant from South Korean, who now resided and worked in Silicon Valley. A whiz kid with all things electrical and mechanical, especially computers, he had been instrumental in helping Harper and Julia Norton escape the converted oil platform prison in the Gulf of Mexico.

The American looked at the wall clock. Only six o'clock Pacific Time, he realized. Allowing for the time difference, Harper told Karmina they had to wait three more hours before he felt sure Seong-ho would be at this place of work.

"So let's order breakfast. When we're done I'll drive you to the harbor. It's quite a tourist attraction," she told him.

Harper smiled back, and they left the café. He did not have the heart to tell her he had been there years before, arriving in something far more exotic than an automobile.

Twelve noon, local time, finally arrived. All Harper had to do was to make a phone call.

While at the café, as well as finding an address and phone number for the South Korean, Harper has also researched ways to place an outbound phone call to the United States. The simplest solution, he concluded, was to find an American tourist that had set up roaming privileges in Cuba. More specifically, a tourist who subscribed to AT&T. Easily enough for Roger Harper. With his mind-reading ability, he was able to located and mentally persuade the owner of a US cell phone to part with it long enough to place a call to Seong-ho and tell him his presence was needed in Havana.

"I cannot go into more details, in case the NSA is listening," he said in all seriousness. "Do you remember the hotel we stayed in last time we were in Cuba together? Just answer me yes or no."

Harper was referring to the Hotel *Ambos Mundos*, a stone's throw from Havana Harbor where they had moored the 'borrowed' Russian submarine after escaping from the Gulf of Mexico prison.

"Yes," the South Korean replied.

"Excellent. By the way, don't rely on credit cards when you come over. Those issued by US banks are not accepted. Bring cash but not in US dollars, as the banks charge a hefty penalty, of ten to fifteen percent, on top of the bad exchange rate. Pick another foreign currency."

"Understood," Seong-ho acknowledged.

"Okay. I'll be waiting in the hotel's foyer over the next few days. Got that?"

"Yes, Harper, but what's this all about?"

"As I said, I can't go into details right now. Less is best. Just trust me." There was a brief moment of silence. "Oh, by the way. Bring with you some American chocolate. That which they make over here tastes excessively sweet."

The cell phone's owner's wife was starting to get agitated with her husband, demanding he ask for his cell phone back

"Gotta go," were Harper's final words before he disconnected the call, not waiting for a reply.

ALLOWING TIME FOR SEONG-HO TO BOOK A TICKET, PACK, GET TO the airport, make at least one interconnecting flight, go through Cuban immigration, and be taxied to the hotel, his earliest arrival would be in twelve hours, Harper calculated. Consequently, once back at the apartment, there was plenty of time to straighten the place up as best they could.

By mid-afternoon, they had finished. Leaving Karmina to catch up with her laundry, Harper settled down on the couch and began reading more of the Spanish phrasebook. Within minutes he was sound asleep.

The American roused himself at 6:00 p.m., showered and dressed. As Karmina prepared dinner, he tried to avoid more of the Cuban's unrelenting questions. However, she did manage to coax from him the fact that Harper was going to meet an old friend. "Don't ask where, and don't ask who he is. The less you know, Karmina, the better," he told her. "End of discussion. And try not to worry. I'll be back as soon as I can."

El Hotel Ambos Mundos, once home to the writer Ernest Hemmingway in the 1930s, had changed little since Harper's last visit.

He seated himself in the reception area, where he had a view of the entryway. After ordered coffee, he settled in behind a copy of *Granma,* the official newspaper published by the Central Committee of the Cuban Communist Party. Notwithstanding the fact the American had no political affiliations, and that he could not read Spanish, he busied himself trying to find strings of words that he recognized from ONE THOUSAND AND ONE PHRASES A TOURIST SHOULD LEARN BEFORE VISITING SPAIN.

Occasionally, when not looking towards the hotel entrance, he found himself dozing off. More coffee did not help.

The wall clock crept slowly around. Ten o'clock. Eleven o'clock. Midnight. Harper wondered if he had been overly optimistic regarding the South Korean's itinerary.

"Sleeping on the job, are we, Harper?" The cheery voice of Seong-ho jolted the American awake. "Wherever did you get that suit? From a dumpster."

Still blurry-eyed, Harper looked at the wall clock. "And good morning to you, Seong-ho. How was your flight?"

"Had to settle for an Economy Class ticket," the South Korean replied. "All the First Class seats were taken. Still, not to worry. I am here. Say, is there somewhere a guy can get something to eat?"

Too early for the hotel's breakfast, Harper hustled up a selection of sandwiches from room service, paying cash and tipping generously. Cold beer was their choice for dessert as Harper told Seong-ho the reason why he had requested his presence in Cuba.

38

THE SOUTH KOREAN INSISTED ON TAKING A ROOM IN THE HOTEL, claiming he needed to sleep. Consequently, using the priest's car for transport, it was ten o'clock before the pair left.

As Harper drove the Chevrolet, still trying to master the subtle intricacies of clutch control and gear changing, Seong-ho, asked, "Tell me again, where are we going?"

"The old part of the city. *You* are going to visit an antique dealer. *I* am going to remain in the car."

"And you want me to purchase a knickknack. Did I hear you correctly? It's a long way to come to buy something I can pick up in Sonoma."

Harper patiently explained, for the second time, "When I purchased the clock, I tricked the owner of the shop into believing he was receiving more money than I gave him. I can't go back in. If he remembers, he will not be too pleased."

"What sort of knicknack are we talking about?" Seong-ho inquired.

"There's a selection of gold chains displayed in the counter cabinet. Choose one you think Julia might like and purchase it for me. That's a good chap."

"That's a good chap," the South Korean mimicked. "You sound just like the British Admiral who rescued us. What was his name?"

"Sir Maxwell Whitmore-Morant. I met his son, William, almost a year ago." The Chevrolet pulled up a block away from the antique shop. "I'll fill you in on the details later. Now off you go, my man. " Harper instructed, once more using his phony British accent.

Seong-ho dropped a small leather-covered box into Harper's lap, after returning to the car.

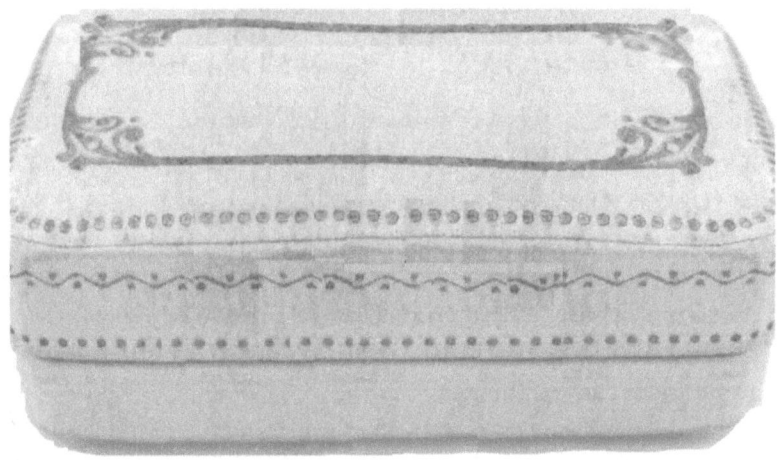

"A present for you. Inside is a gold chain. You just have to add the key. The jewelry box adds the finishing touch, don't you think? You should enclose a note as well, telling Julia you're safe," the South Korean suggested.

"I'm not sure that's a good idea, Seong-ho. What am I supposed to say? *Dear Jules, I'm fine. See you sometime, but I don't know when.* That sounds somewhat lame if you ask me."

After lifting the lid, removing the cotton padding, and inspecting the chain, Harper discovered a name and address stamped on the base of the box.

PALLARES

CALLE 33 ESQ. 4

VEDADO

"Mmm. There's a chance this label might give Jules a clue that I'm still alive. That should be message enough."

"If she realizes the gift if from you."

"Who else would send Jules jewelry? She's bound to figure it out," Harper confidently concluded.

The American selected first gear, causing the transmission to make a loud grinding noise. As he let out the clutch, the Chevrolet Bel Air leaped forward. The Korean deftly caught the box, which Harper had casually placed on the dashboard moments earlier.

"Would you like me to drive?"

"It's okay, thanks. Sit back and relax."

"With you behind the wheel? Fat chance," Seong-ho replied. "Where are we going next? Back to the hotel?"

"Nope. To an apartment. I want you to meet a new friend of mine. Her name is Karmina. And before you ask, I'm not cheating on Julia."

"How did you meet her?" Seong-ho inquired as Harper swerved to avoid a bicyclist who thought he had the run of the road.

"No doubt she will tell you herself. Now, less chitchatting, if you don't mind. It's been a long time since I've driven a car. I need to concentrate."

Seong-ho could not suppress a laugh. "That is more than obvious, Harper. A word of advice; don't give up the day job."

39

HARPER PARKED THE CAR IN THE SQUARE OVERLOOKED BY THE apartment. Having climbed to the third floor, he was surprised to find not only Karmina inside but Federico as well. The Brazilian explained he had badgered the doctor for an early discharge from the hospital, after his girlfriend telephoned to give him the news about Father Marcolata's death, and that the presbytery was no longer a place to stay.

Harper clasped his arms around Federico's shoulders by way of a greeting, and whispered in his ear, "This place may be wired with hidden microphones. Say nothing to indicate I have brought a guest and quietly tell Karmina to do the same. Nod if you understand."

Federico nodded. Everyone, except Seong-ho, sat down. Ever prepared for such eventualities, with a pocket spy bug detector, the Korean began sweeping the room for listening devices. Meanwhile, the American passed a piece of notepaper to Karmina The message he had just penned read,

```
When I ask you questions, play along.
Show this note to Federico as well.
```

"Karmina, is there someplace overlooking this apartment where you can set up surveillance? I want to find out if anyone suspicious is watching to see who comes and goes."

"I could ask the neighbor across the square if I can use his place. He probably wouldn't mind, especially if I bring him a packet of cigarettes," Federico's girlfriend replied.

"Good idea. Be prepared to stay a day or two. If you *do* see anyone hanging around, I want you to follow them when they leave." In particular, Harper was alluding to the German muscle that had hit the Brazilian over the head. "Stay on their tail. I want to find out where they are based. It might lead us to their boss. ¿Entiendes?" he added, practicing his Spanish.

The Korean silently waved his arms to attract their attention. *I've found the bug* he mouthed, pointing to the table lamp that had conveniently remained upright during the tossing of the apartment.

"Sí," Karmina responded as if nothing had been discovered, "but the Lada is still parked near the museum."

"I forgot," the American admitted. "Maybe you should go get your car first."

"Hold on a second, Harper. What will you and I be doing? We are not staying here, surely?" Federico asked.

"No, we are not." The American gave a broad smile, for, predictably, the Brazilian had not needed any scripting, always on the lookout for a story. "Tomorrow morning, we are going to take a drive to the Marina, charter a fishing boat, and pretend to be Ernest Hemingway for a day. Who knows, Federico, you might land a marlin or even a barracuda."

Thirty-three feet long, the *Costa Azul* provided enough room for up to ten passengers to spend a day deep sea fishing. Included in the charter was gear, bait, snacks, beverages, and a captain named José Enriques Ruiz.

Today the only two *clientela* were Harper and Federico. After a little instruction, both men had landed a couple of moderately-sized bonefish, each weighing between eight and twelve pounds apiece. Not quite the prize-winning catch they had been contemplating.

Harper sat back, sunglasses and sombrero protecting him from the glare of the sun, wondering if bonefish was the only fish he was going to catch today. He had not noticed anyone following them to the Marina, or as they chartered the boat. "Perhaps this little excursion is a waste of time," he said out loud.

"Not at all, Mr. Harper. Thank you for the invite." Harper swiveled his fishing chair, unbuckling his harness at the same time. "Don't bother to get up, Mr. Harper. Not until we have had a little chat."

"Daniels. Doctor Daniels."

"We meet again, Mr. Harper. A little older than when we first met, but I pride myself that I am aging well."

"What are you doing here?"

"We have an old score to settle, Mr. Harper. You have been a thorn in my flesh that has been festering for some time. The fact that you are here in Cuba saves me the trouble of looking for you." A thick-set, brute of a man stepped out of the wheelhouse, cracking his knuckles. "Everything in order, Hans?"

"*Ja, Herr Doktor.* The captain is below, sleeping."

With a simper of inner satisfaction, "Like a baby, I trust," Daniels replied. Federico got up from his chair. "And where does our journalist friend think he's going?"

"To get a beer," Federico replied. "Would you like one?"

"I don't trust you. Sit back down. Hans, do the honors if you please."

"The cooler is amidship, on the port side," Harper volunteered.

The bodyguard made his way forward, stopping when he could not find the container. "Where is *das Flaschenbier* kept?" he shouted.

"Let me show him," Federico suggested.

This time Daniels did not object. The Brazilian, choosing the starboard side, walked towards the bow. Opening the cooler, he selected three beers and handed them to the German-speaking bodyguard who had joined him.

Hans returned to the stern.

"Not drinking yourself, *señor* Federico?" Daniels called out, seemingly unconcerned that the Brazilian had remained by the cooler. "Your name is Federico? I'm sure I've got that right. It is surprising what information a hidden microphone in that young lady's apartment can convey."

"Doctors orders," Federico replied, unfazed. "After my little bang on the head, no alcohol for a week or two, I was told."

"You should change your doctor," Daniels responded with a chuckle. "If you're wondering how I found you so easily, Harper, after eavesdropping on the little powwow with your friends yesterday, it was not too difficult to ensure you chose this boat for charter." Daniels skillfully popped his beer bottle open by hooking the edge of the cap against the gunwale and smacking the top with the flat of his other hand. Then raising it high, he proposed a toast. "Here's to meeting old friends. *¡Salud!*"

The doctor took a swig of beer. Purposely, Harper botched opening his own bottle. When Daniels offered to assist, Federico surreptitiously took a couple of steps to the side.

"By the way," the doctor continued, "if you are thinking of trying to play any of your mind games, forget it. Thanks to unique training, both Hans and I are immune to your probing. Now, where were we? Oh, yes, toasting old friends. We should include absent friends as well. Here is to my poor brother, Robin. *Prost!*" Daniels took another swig of beer. "You didn't have to kill him, you know. Spoiling his fun, stealing the artwork, should have been enough."

The American's eyes widened at the realization that the brother's last name was Hyde.

"Robin Hyde was your brother? How come you are calling yourself Daniels?"

"Proper chatterbox, aren't you, Harper. Stalling for time; is that it? Won't do you any good. Once I've done here, you will become nothing other than fish bait."

"Indulge me, Daniels. Think of it as a condemned man's last wish."

Federico sidestepped some more, unnoticed by either the doctor or bodyguard, until he was hidden by the wheelhouse.

"Very well. No one can say I'm not generous to a fault. Throughout Junior and High School, my brother, Robin, and I kept the same surname. He was a year younger than me but much brighter. His education was fast-tracked. We graduated at the same time, applied for the same medical school, and both got accepted. We enrolled in the same courses, attended the same lectures and seminars. That's when it became a problem. The professors, real sticks-in-the-mud they were, insisted on addressing all the male students by there last names. Whenever *Hyde* was called out, if Robin and I were together, we both answered."

The Brazilian silently moved again, stopping when he reached the fish locker. Noiselessly, he lifted the lid.

"It came to the point of being embarrassing. That is when

Robin came up with the idea that one of us should change their last name. On the flip of a coin, that was me."

"Why choose Daniels?" Harper asked.

"That was a spur of the moment thing. When we were kids, we both took part in a Sunday School production, *Daniel In The Lion's Den*. Robin portrayed the lion. I played Daniel. I'm sure that little brain of yours can figure out the rest."

"Well, you've filled in some of the blanks, *Herr Doktor*. It will help me in stopping your criminal activities."

"And what crimes are those?"

"Kidnappings on the island, that started twenty years ago, for starters."

Daniels laughed. "Harper, Harper. You have it all wrong. My late father takes the credit for the earlier ones, may God rest his soul."

"Your father had no soul, Daniels. Neither did your brother, and neither do you."

"Now, now, Harper. Don't be so self-righteous. Remember the old adage *like father, like son*, and you will realize that I am merely carrying on his life-long calling."

"You're a cold-blooded bastard, Daniels. Do you know that?"

"Calm yourself, Harper. If that priest taught you a prayer or two, now is the time to say them."

"So it was you who tortured and killed Father Marcolata. Why?"

Federico slowly bent down and picked up a bonefish in each hand.

"Not me personally, Harper. Hans, here, takes the credit for that. Our fathers were close friends when they lived in *Colonia Barón*, Argentina. That's where he was born. As to why; you have something of mine, I want back."

"As soon as we return to shore, I'll have the police arrest you both."

Daniels let out a hearty laugh. "Harper, you should have been a comedian. You, an escaped fugitive, are going to get me arrested?"

Creeping forward, the Brazilian positioned himself so that with one deft step, he would have Daniels and Hans in clear view.

"But enough of this small talk. Time for you, Mr. Harper, to meet your Maker. Hans, if you'd be so kind, please do the honors."

"*Meine Freude, Doktor* [My pleasure, Doctor]."

As the bodyguard stepped towards Harper, Federico took aim. With all his might, he flung a ten-pound fish and then another. Both men were struck on the back of the head and collapsed to the deck.

"Well done, Federico. You should become a pitcher for the Boston Red Socks."

"Thanks, Harper, but I'll stick with journalism, if it's all the same to you. What shall we do with these two?" the Brazilian asked. "Throw them over the side?"

"No," Harper replied. "I'm not going to stoop to their level. Find some rope and tie them up. Then we'll head back to the Marina. But first, I'm going below to see how Captain Ruiz is doing."

HANS WRAPPED ON THE OPEN DOOR OF DANIELS' OFFICE BEFORE entering. "Any new developments from Harper and his friend since we last met?" he was asked.

"*Nein, Herr Doktor.* They went back to the apartment belonging to the journalist's girlfriend. We watched the place for a while, but observed nothing of interest."

"Perhaps they are waiting for divine inspiration, Hans. If they are hoping to find this place, they'll need plenty of that. Anything else to report?"

"Yes, indeed, sir. *Der IT-Techniker* [The IT technician] has cracked the password to the Brazilian's computer. He found mention of the carriage clock given by *Presidente* Batista to *Captán* Ventura."

Daniels scoffed. "That's old news, Hans. You took it from the apartment after confronting the journalist, remember?"

"Unquestionably, it is the same clock, *Herr Doktor.* However, Ramírez references where it was found; an antique shop on the corner of *Calle 33* and *4.*"

"Really?" Referring to another of his henchmen, the doctor

continued, "You should get Bernhart to pay the owner a visit and ascertain when Federico made the purchase."

"Bernhart already has, sir. It wasn't the Brazilian who acquired the clock, however. It was an American."

"Did Bernhart get a description?" Daniels asked.

"*Señor* Pallares was extremely vague on that, sir. He would say one thing, the next moment changing his mind, and say something completely different."

"Harper! It had to be Harper using his mind probing ability to confuse Pallares. Did the man say anything at all useful?"

"The proprietor did mention another man came into the shop the day before we had the confrontation with Harper on the fishing boat. Pallares said this man looked to be Vietnamese or Korean."

"I don't see the connection, Hans."

"Maybe it's nothing, *Herr Doktor,* but the owner said he too had a North American accent."

"Did this Asian buy anything?"

"A gold chain and a jewelry box; paid for in Canadian dollars."

"So what? How is a Canadian tourist purchasing a memento of his trip to Cuba connected to Harper?"

"With respect, *Herr Doktor,* you may be wrong. The antique dealer showed Bernhart a receipt the tourist had dropped on his way out of the shop. It was for sandwiches purchased at *El Hotel Ambos Mundos.* I checked it out and spoke to the night porter. He remembers the man because later he booked a room and stayed until morning. The hotel records show his name as Seong-ho Moon."

"Seong-ho Moon? Well, I never. What a small world we live in, Hans. *Herr* Moon was one of the internees on the oil platforms. His parents were from South Korea if I remember correctly. He must have escaped with Roger Harper and Julia Norton. Anything else?"

"One of the staff recalled someone waiting in the hotel lobby and meeting up with this *Herr* Moon in the early hours of the morning," Hans replied. "You'll never guess who that person was."

"Harper, obviously," Daniels replied. "I doubt this was just a reunion for old times' sake. What brought them together, I wonder?"

"I don't know, *Herr Doktor*, but that same day the gold chain and jewelry box were purchased. I sent Günter to the airport to find out if Moon has left the country."

There was a pause.

"Go on, man," Daniels demanded, impatiently. "This is not a bedtime story you are narrating."

"Günter spoke to our contact in Immigration Control. *Herr* Moon flew to Miami, Florida. From there, he took an American Airlines flight to Savannah, Georgia. However, his inbound trip originated in California; San Francisco International Airport."

The doctor stroked his chin. "What made him decided to go to Savannah is the big question?"

Hans stood there, grinning

"From the look on your face, Hans, you doubtless have the answer."

"Indeed I do, sir. I placed Günter on the corporate jet, to find out."

"I knew I could rely on you, Hans. Always able to use your initiative without having to ask. Has Günter reported back?"

"*Ja, Herr Doktor*. It was not too difficult to find the hotel where the Korean is staying. From there, Günter started following him. For the past two days, Moon has parked himself outside a Savannah residence."

"And the owner of this residence is?" Daniels asked.

"No one we know, sir. But two doors down, that's a different story. It's the home of a Mrs. Cordelia Montgomery, the aunt of Julia Harper, née Norton."

"Harper's wife. Interesting. Do you think he was sent there to ensure their safety?"

Hans laughed. "If that was the intention, why remain in the car. He would be better off staying inside the house."

"Plainly, an amateur." Daniels sat back in his chair and put his finger-tips together forming a bridge, thinking. After a minute, he continued, "What if there's another reason Moon journeyed to *Frau* Montgomery's humble abode. We need to be proactive, Hans. Send Conrad White and Kirt Mitchell to Savannah. Julia Harper knows them both. I believe now is a good time to pay her a social visit."

4 2

SITTING IN A RENTED TOYOTA COROLLA TWENTY YARDS UP THE road, facing toward the entrance of Aunt Cordelia's plantation-style home, the Korean was suffering the third day of a stakeout. His limbs ached, he needed something to eat, and, more pressing, he needed to use the bathroom.

There had always been at least one adult in the Savannah residence at all times. This morning was no exception. Cordelia had left the house twenty minutes earlier, pushing a pram, with Oliver skipping along beside her. Seong-ho had heard the Aunt talking about the park and the swings. *Presumably, that was where they are going,* he told himself. *I should have at least an hour before they return.*

Wondering whether or not Julia would leave, he endured the frustration for five more minutes.

She did not.

Maybe I missed her, he thought, having dozed off a short while ago. Seong-ho, deciding his surveillance could not continue forever, lifted his cell phone from its holster, ensured the settings would block his caller ID, and dialed the house phone.

It rang and rang until it went to voicemail. Without leaving a message, the Korean hung up.

Exiting the car, Seong-ho looked behind to check that the Aunt and the children were not returning early.

All clear.

Walking at a brisk pace, he opened the latch gate. Not using the garden path, he skirted the lawn, keeping close to the hedging. He caught the intense citrus-like fragrance wafting on the breeze as he approached the front porch.

There he froze.

A woman lay on an outdoor couch, eyes closed, her bosom heaving gently with each shallow breath. Seong-ho took a moment to look into her face. *Julia. Older than when we last met by ten years or so.* The Korean crept past, willing every creaking board on the decking to be quiet.

He tried the door.

Thanks to Oliver's idea of a prank, the boy had released the snib causing the latch to self-lock.

Never one to arrive unprepared, the Korean pulled a lock picking kit from inside his jacket. In no time, he was standing in the entrance hall. The only sound was the constant tick-tock of a grandfather clock.

Remembering Harper's explicit instruction, he tip-toed along the hallway until he found the dining room. The next item Seong-ho removed from his jacket was the gift-wrapped box purchased from the antique shop in Havana. He placed it in the center of the dining table.

Next, he removed his wallet and took out the folded piece of paper that was the formula Harper had discovered in the asylum basement. Having received no specific instruction except to place it in a safe place, the Korean looked around the room. Directly opposite the window, on top of a sideboard, there was a glass cabinet. Seong-ho contemplated slipping the paper inside one of the china teapots on display. Not a satisfactory hiding place if Aunt Cordelia used the teapot on special occasions when guests visited.

Seong-ho elected to try another room.

Entering the parlor, he observed a pair of oil paintings, one on each side of the fireplace. If Julia had been there, she might have told him that art connoisseurs categorized the abstract concept depicted as *Altermodern*. The Korean had little interest in modern art. Nevertheless, tucking the formula behind the right-hand frame was an excellent solution.

The grandfather clock began chiming the quarter-hour. *Time to go*, Seong-ho told himself but not before he had availed himself of the facilities.

43

"JULIA," CORDELIA SPOKE SOFTLY. "WE'RE HOME."

"How long was I asleep," Julia asked as she roused herself from the outdoor couch.

"I don't know. We came back from the park over an hour ago."

"Where are Ophelia and Olly?" Julia inquired.

"Ophelia is sleeping in her crib, and Oliver is making cookies. Come on through, when you're ready. I am about to see how much cleanup your son has left me."

There was the sound of running feet. Oliver appeared, clutching a small package wrapped in brown paper. "Look what I found on the dining room table. There's no name on it. Do you think it's for me?"

"Why don't you open it, Olly? There may be a note inside."

Not bothering to break the embossed red seal, he boy tore away the wrapping, revealing a small box, covered in soft leather etched with gold-leaf border patterns.

Oliver opened the lid to find, placed between layers of cotton padding, a key and a gold chain. Oliver picked up the key for his mother and great-aunt to see.

"What is it for?" Julia wondered out loud.

"To open a cabinet or a drawer, perhaps," Cornelia suggested. "Why someone should leave it here, I have no idea."

"Me neither," Julia replied, threading the chain through the eye at the top of the key. She put the chain over her head. "Then again, it makes a distinctive necklace."

"If you like that sort of thing," her aunt responded with a snicker. "Not to my taste, however. Now, if it had been a string of pearls, that would be a different story."

"On the face of it, there has been an intruder," Cordelia concluded. "I think I'll go check if anything has been taken." She picked up the empty jewelry box. Before going indoors, she reminded her niece that cookies were available in the kitchen.

"Thanks. I'll be there, in a minute," Julia replied, and then, turning to her son, she asked him to check on his sister.

Oliver did as he was told, leaving his mother alone to stare at the magnolia tree whose olive-green leaves and white flowers were being teased by the breeze. Subconsciously Julia fingered the key, trying to make a connection.

In the dining room, nothing seemed to be missing, or in any other part of the house for that matter. Entering the parlor, Cordelia walked to the fireplace. After putting the cornsilk-colored leather box on the mantelpiece, she stepped away. Noticing one of the two paintings Julia had shipped from her Dubai villa was lopsided, the aunt reached out a hand and made a slight adjustment.

She never considered the fact that, earlier in the day, both paintings were perfectly straight and level. If she had made a closer inspection, she might have noticed a small envelope secreted behind the artwork. But she did not.

If she had looked inside the key box and removed the layers of cotton wool, she would have read the name and address stamped inside the base. But she did not.

All this time, Julia, standing on the front stoop, was wondering who had sent the gifts and why. A hummingbird flew from the magnolia tree, traversing the lawn to take nectar from a flowering trumpet creeper. As the bird crossed the footpath leading to the main road, for a second, Julia vaguely recalled the image of a man, short in stature, walking away from her as she lay on the couch. Except for a slight limp as he favored his right leg, there were no distinguishing features to identify the person.

From somewhere, I know that man. A forgotten memory tried to surface from the deep crevices of her mind. *I'm sure I know him.*

The porch door opened, and then banged closed as Oliver stepped through. "Mom, Ophelia is crying. I think she needs to be fed."

"Thanks, Olly," Julia replied, her moment of introspection over.

44

"Stop walking back and forth, Harper. You are getting on my nerves," Federico protested. "Do something constructive like lean to speak Spanish?"

"Spanish? Half the world speaks English. I can't see the point."

"Half the world's population speaks Chinese, you mean. At least, sit down."

"Leave me alone, Federico. I'm thinking."

"You can sit down and do that," the Brazilian suggested.

Harper took no notice.

A couple of minutes later, he stopped his pacing. Now standing in front of a map of Cuba pinned to the wall, which showed a route marked out with a felt-tipped pen, he suggested, "We need to drive out there and see for ourselves. How long do you think that will take, Federico?"

Realizing he would get no peace, with a sigh, the Brazilian left the desk and walked over to the map. Using a ruler, he measured the distance. "Two hundred and sixty kilometers. From here, about four hours. Maybe longer, depending on traffic."

Two hundred and sixty kilometers was as far as Karmina's

neighbor, riding his motorcycle, had tracked two men in a black Mercedes.

Yesterday, looking down from the neighbor's apartment, she had spotted a heavily built man, hair crew cut and wearing sunglasses, get out of the vehicle parked below. He walked around the corner and disappeared. After a few minutes, the car drove away only to return an hour later. The passenger reappeared and swapped seats with the driver. The latter, slightly smaller in stature, with a baseball cap pulled down hard on his head, followed the same pattern, disappearing around the same corner.

Federico's girlfriend realized that the men were taking turns watching her apartment. Thirty minutes later, the Mercedes was back, picking up the baseball guy before driving off.

Why the surveillance lasted such a short time, Karmina could not fathom. Maybe their boss called them away? Having eavesdropped on the group's conversation about her acting as a lookout, perhaps it was an elaborate trick?

However, the Cuban had a trick of her own. Despite her original proposal to use the Lada, Karmina realized by the time she had descended the stairs and started her vehicle, the other car would be long gone. Instead, she had her neighbor hide close by, ready to mount a motorcycle and follow. All it needed was Karmina putting two fingers in his mouth and whistling. The chase was on, or, as Harper might have quoted, *the game's afoot*.

And that is what the map showed. The Mercedes had driven aimless around the backstreets of Havana for ten minutes, presumably checking to see if the Lada was behind them. Then it headed east, along *Autopista Nacional*, the motorway that linked the capital with Guantánamo. Reaching *Aguada de Pasajeros*, the vehicle then turned southeast, taking State Highway *Circuito Sur*. Passing *Real Campina* and *Yaguaramas*, at *Cienfuegos*, the car turned south following *12* for twenty miles. Next, for no apparent reason, it took the mountain road east that climbed to an elevation of 2,600 feet. All this time, the motorcyclist followed, staying back to avoid being spotted.

Then, at the farming village of *La Sierrata*, disaster. The motorcycle ran out of gasoline.

"So, where do you think the Mercedes was heading?" Harper asked.

"Beats me," Federico replied. "For all I know, the whole thing was a wild goose chase."

"Or possibly not," the American contradicted. "The Mercedes was defiantly heading east. My guess is, at some point, the occupants became aware the motorcycle was following them. That's when they decided to take the mountain road. It's a long shot, but I still think we should drive there and see for ourselves."

"Agreed," Federico replied, "but we should start in the morning. It is too late in the day to go now. Learn to relax. Sit down next to Karmina and watch television."

"In Spanish? As if I'd understand a word."

"Then read a book."

"All the books in this place are in Spanish or Portuguese," Harper reminded the Brazilian.

"There's an English edition of *War and Peace*, somewhere," Federico, who had returned to the desk chair, called out.

"Thanks a lot, pal. Tolstoy is my favorite author," the American responded, sarcastically. "Besides, Seong-ho should have contacted me by now and given me an update on his Savannah venture. Something's wrong, I know."

"Give him time," Federico suggested.

"Why don't I use the wall phone and call him?" Harper suggested.

"Not the smartest thing to do, Harper. If someone is tapping Karmina's phone, they will overhear every word."

"Why would anyone bother?" the American asked.

Federico stooped typing on the computer he had borrowed from Karmina. "Have you forgotten, Harper, that this is Cuba?"

The American sat down on the couch. Arms folded, he gloomily stared at the television, wishing he were back with his family.

"Harper, you don't believe me, do you?"

"Believe what?" the American responded testily.

"Pick up the phone and listen. Don't dial or say anything."

"Whatever for?"

"Just do it, and you will find out."

For want of something more constructive to do, Harper complied. After a few seconds, he put the handset back in its cradle.

"Well?" the Brazilian asked. "What did you learn?"

"You mean the crackling sound? Isn't that just the Cuban telephone network?"

"More likely, someone is tapping the line."

"Seriously," Harper responded. "Who would want to do that?"

"Various governments. You're spoiled for choice. Cuba. Russia. The United States. That's almost a given. Even my own country."

"For what reason?" Harper asked.

"I'm a reporter. Need I say more?"

The American shook his head in disbelief. "A reporter that has a hack column in a tin-pot newspaper. Who is partway through an unpublished biography of Batista. And someone who can't keep his girlfriend's fridge stocked with beer."

"I'm only saying, that's all," Federico replied defensively. "And we mustn't forget to add your friend Daniels to the list."

"That's hard to do. *Herr Doktor* has become a permanent pain in my butt." The American stood up and resumed his pacing of the room.

"For heaven's sake, Harper, I'm trying to work, here. Why don't you take the priest's car keys, find an Internet café, and see if Seong-ho has left you any messages?"

"Okay. I will." The American took the keys. "Perhaps you'd be so kind as to come with me, Karmina?"

"If you're looking for a date, buddy, may I remind you she's spoken for?"

"No, Federico, I am not. If you must know, I can't get a handle on the vehicle's confounded stick shift. I need Karmina as my driver."

45

ONCE IN THE CAR, KARMINA ASKED, "DO YOU TRULY NEED A chauffeur, Harper? When necessary, you have managed to drive yourself."

"You're right, I don't," the American replied. "But, I do need you to keep a lookout while I'm in the café using the Internet."

As she drove, Karmina remarked, "Those comments about phone tapping has got you paranoid, Harper. Federico was winding you up, that's all. Don't take things so seriously."

"So how come the noises on the phone line? That wasn't my imagination."

The Cuban shrugged her shoulders. "As you said earlier, it's probably the network."

"Better safe than sorry, Karmina. I have a feeling Daniels has his fingers in many pies. I don't trust anybody I don't know personally. Come on. Head along *Calle Dragones*. I'm anxious to know what Seong-ho is up to."

The Korean answered Harper's email within minutes. He confirmed he had left the key and formula at Cordial's house. Immediately, Harper replied, telling Seong-ho about the confrontation with Daniels on the chartered fishing boat.

The reaction was almost predictable:

```
You let Daniels go? In light of what that
monster did to us, I can't believe it. You
should have treated the doctor to a swim
back to shore, with lead weights around his
ankles.
```

Harper calmly responded, justifying his reason for doing so.

```
I left him alive to see what he'll do next.
I don't think he knows that I found the
formula. There's only a vague one-line
reference by Esteban Ventura in his journal.
```

Seong-ho come back with the question, *Do you wanted me back in Cuba?*

Harper typed his reply,

```
No. I'll email you if I need you again. Go
back to California. Thanks for your help,
buddy. Be safe. Bye.
```

A few seconds after he hit the email *send* icon, Karmina came rushing into the café.

"Hey, Harper; what was the name of the sea captain, the one who chartered you and Federico the fishing boat?"

"José Enriques Ruiz. Why?"

"I've just heard on the car's radio," she said breathlessly, "Captain Ruiz's body has washed ashore near the small town of *Nuevo Mariel*, twenty miles west of the Marina."

46

THE NEXT DAY, HARPER, FEDERICO, AND KARMINA DROVE TO THE location where the black Mercedes was last sighted.

The Brazilian had bought with him his camera that had a telescopic lens, and a pair of binoculars. Both, he claimed, were for bird watching. The latter Harper had to his eyes, looking out to sea, as he stood on the edge of the mountain road.

"Anything interesting?" Karmina asked, still sitting in the driver's seat of the Chevrolet.

Harper responded, "A couple of fishing boats and a tramp steamer, that is all. On the coastal road, a tanker truck is all I am seeing. A twenty-two wheeler, if I'm not mistaken. "

Federico swung his camera's telescopic lens in the direction the American was looking. "That's a brute of a thing. I've not seen anything quite like it on the island before."

"It's got to be hauling twelve thousand gallons, or more, if fully ladened."

"You know about tankers, then, Harper?" Federico asked.

"My grandfather was a truck driver. As a teenager, I would sometimes ride with him during vacations. I wonder where that rig is going?"

"To a place that needs its supply of liquid replenishing," Karmina suggested, in a flippant manner.

"Ha, ha, very droll," Harper responded. "What about you, Federico; do you see anything else?"

The Brazilian, still using his camera lens as a magnifier, answered, "Nothing of interest. Wait a minute. There's a flock of turkey vultures spiraling upwards to gain altitude, over there." He pointed. "The birds take on the appearance of water boiling in a pot. We birdwatchers use the term kettle when we see that."

"Enough with the factoid," Harper replied, regarding Federico's observation as irrelevant to their mission. Still looking for something that may give them a clue as to why the tanker was in the vicinity, he panned the binoculars past the inlet to *Bahia de Cienfuegos* [Cienfuegos Bay]. If the American had known, he too might have shared the pointless piece of information that on his second voyage to the Americas, Christopher Columbus visited the bay in 1494. Instead, he remarked on the cluster of what looked like derelict buildings, too far away to pick out any detail.

After listening to the two men's remarks, Karmina interjected, saying, "This is a complete waste of time. We should start heading back to Havana."

Federico concurred, jumping into the front passenger seat before the American could stake a claim. Karmina smiled, finally getting some attention, and turned on the ignition. After slipping the vehicle into gear, she did a K-turn.

"Come on, Harper. Hop in," Federico said jocularly. "It's a long walk back to town."

They retraced their route, debating whether or not to stop and eat at they drove through *Cienfuegos*.

"See those dark clouds gathering out to sea. A storm is coming," Federico predicted. "We should go back to the city straight away. Cubans drive like crazies, even when it's raining, and I don't want to be involved in an accident."

With that compelling argument, Karmina drove on for another ten and a half miles.

As they passed a side road, on their left leading to the coast, Harper glanced in that direction. "Slow down, Karmina. That's the second road tanker I've seen today, and it's similar to the first."

The young woman pulled off the road, and everyone looked. A twenty-two wheeled tanker truck was doggedly negotiating its way down the gradient, trailing a cloud of dust.

Harper grabbed the binoculars. "No marking on the rear, so it can't be carrying hazardous materials," he concluded.

The Brazilian scoffed. "This is Cuba, my friend. It could be full of liquid chlorine or corn syrup, and you'd never know. If you're expecting Hazmat placards plastered all over the place, you are sorely mistaken."

"What's down there?" Karmina inquired.

Federico pulled the map out of the car's glove compartment. "The road leads to the bay's inlet, but there's nothing of interest there that I can see."

"Give me the map, please, Federico."

After a quick examination, Harper continued. "Except for some derelict buildings, which I saw from the mountain road. We should take a closer look."

As the American spoke, the first drops of rain began. There was a scramble to raise the convertible's soft top.

"We should leave?" the Brazilian persisted.

"Rain or no rain, I vote we take the time to see what's down there," Harper responded.

"Me too," said Karmina, using her casting vote.

47

AFTER A MILE, THE UNMETALLED ROAD GREW STEEPER AND BEGAN A lazy zigzag down the slope. Except for the tire tracks of heavy vehicles, there was still little to see. As the rain became more incessant, the wipers struggled to clear the windscreen. Karmina began to wish she had voted to return to the apartment.

Suddenly, over the ceaseless drumming of water on the Chevrolet's vinyl roof, the sound of a blaring horn could be heard, causing the American to swivel his body and looked out of the rear window. Another supertanker was barreling down on them. Despite the rain, Harper could see into the cab. The driver's face was one broad malicious leer, characteristic of a psychotic maniac intent on killing someone.

With rocky outcrops on one side of the narrow track and a drop on the other, there was nowhere to go.

"Karmina put your foot down," Harper yelled, now clearly seeing the whites of the driver's eyes.

"Faster, *mi amor* [my love]," Federico urged.

"In these conditions? I could run off the road if I'm not careful," his girlfriend replied.

"Move!" Harper screamed. "We're out of time! It's practically on top of us."

As Karmina floored the gas pedal, the rear wheels of the Bel Air spun. Instantaneously, as the tires regained traction, the car leaped forward, opening up a small gap between the two vehicles.

There was a grinding noise as the truck driver hastily changed up a gear, allowing the twenty-two wheeler to pick up speed. Within seconds the truck was again within inches of their rear bumper. Harper decided it was either the tanker or the car. Closing his eyes, he sent a mental message telling the truck driver to turn the steering wheel to the right, which would send the tanker towards the rocky outcrops.

No response.

When Harper looked again, he could see the driver was grinning. As he gunned the engine, the man tapped the helmet on his head.

"Holy cow," the American declared, realizing the headgear, similar to that of the guards at GITMO, could block an intrusive telepath.

The truck nudged the back of the car, causing the vehicle to slew from side to side. Karmina struggled to keep control.

"You son of a bitch!" Harper yelled. "If it's a wrestling match you want, we'll see who wins."

When in the Clock Tower of London's Big Ben, the American had discovered, as well as being able to read minds and influence people's actions, he could move objects. Applying intense concentration, he willed the tanker's steering wheel to turn towards the drop-off.

The driver yanked it back. Doubling his effort, Harper tried again.

The tractor's offside wheels left the track. Almost in slow motion, the semi slipped sideways and then began to topple on its side. Groaning metal. A bursting tire. The noise was nothing like the occupants of the car had heard before.

The three watched as the tanker continued down the slope, only stopping once it had reached the gully.

"Where's the explosion?" Federico asked.

"This is not the movies," Harper replied. "But I'd be interested to know what liquid it's carrying."

To that end, all three got out of the vehicle to take a look.

Leaving Karmina watching from the track, the two men scrambled down the slope. Reaching the tanker, the American walked to the gaping hole in its side.

"It's water," was Harper's verdict having first sniffed, then touched, and finally tasted the fluid that was spilling from a rupture in the cylinder.

Federico, who had been checking to see if the drive was dead, walked neared. "That makes no sense. "

"Perhaps our Doctor Daniels is refilling his swimming pool," Harper responded with a straight face.

"It's distilled water," the Brazilian clarified, after checking for himself. "No smell, no taste, completely clear."

"The plot thickens." Harper's announcement coincided with a slow roll of thunder. The rain increased in ferocity. "We should leave right now," he yelled over the noise.

"What about the truck diver?" Karmina shouted when the two men regained the track. "We cannot just leave him."

"His friends will take care of him, I'm sure," Harper responded.

"How do you know that?" the Brazilian asked. "He could remain there for days."

"Look towards the coast, Federico. Can't you see a vehicle's headlights moving our way?"

"I see what you mean," the Brazilian replied. "Best we depart before it gets here."

Once back at the car, Federico commandeered the driver's seat, insisting he was accustomed to driving in heavy rain. Harper, having no reason to dispute the Brazilian assertion, hunkered down in the back, closed his eyes, and tried to sleep, deciding that he had had enough excitement for one day.

THE SOUNDS OF CAR DOORS CLOSING AND PEOPLE TALKING DREW Oliver to his bedroom window. Looking down onto the driveway, he saw a man removing luggage from the truck and a woman carrying what might have been a boxed cake. Both appeared to be about five years younger than his mother.

A girl, slightly taller and perhaps a year older than Oliver, stepped out of the rear door of the car, followed by a dog which delighted in running around in circles on the lawn, yapping for all it was worth.

"Olly, your new friend has arrived," Julia called from the hallway.

"I'll choose my own friends; thank you very much," the boy muttered to himself.

"Oliver, did you hear me? Come downstairs, now."

"Yes, Mom," he called back, before going to his bed, pulling on a pair of knee-length socks, and slipping into shoes that required lacing up. "All this nonsense, because we have visitors," he continued, complaining to himself as he made his way down the stairs.

"Olly, there you are. Say hello to my cousin Hope, and her husband George. And this is their daughter, Spencer."

"Hello," Oliver responded unenthusiastically.

"Woof, woof," the dog barked, not wanting to be left out.

"And this is Shadow," said Spencer. "I named him Shadow because he follows me everywhere."

"A schoolfriend of mine has a dog who is always chasing its shadow. Does *your* dog do that?" Oliver asked.

Spencer scowled back; she did not like smarty-pants remarks. However, not to be outplayed, she responded, "You have friends, do you, Oliver? *My* dog is very selective about choosing *his* friends. Isn't that right, Shadow?"

"Why don't you all go into the dining room?" Cordelia suggested, "Lunch is almost ready. I've just taken the friend chicken off the stove."

Oliver listened to the adults taking as the meal progressed. He learned that Spencer's parents were missionaries, about to spend a year at the Santa Cruz Christian Learning Center in Bolivia. Their daughter, when not at boarding school, would be spending her vacations at Cordelia's house. Shadow as well, Oliver assumed.

The mutt having revised its first impression of the boy, was making itself at home, accepting scraps of meat sneaked under the table.

Lunch lasted over an hour. At the first opportunity, the children excused themselves and went outside to play Frisbee. Shadow proved a natural, catching the plastic plate every time. Eventually, the threesome grew tired and came indoors.

"You two look hot," their great-aunt told them. "Would you like some lemonade? I'll get a pitcher from the refrigerator. Shadow, come with me, and I'll give you a bowl of cold water."

Later in the afternoon, Julia suggested they all play cards.

"Only if we can play *Go Fish*," Spencer stipulated. "I'm rather good at that," she announced proudly.

Good or not, Oliver had the uncanny knack of asking everyone for cards held in their hands, hardly ever having to *Go Fish*.

After three rounds, Spencer decided she did not want to play anymore, convinced Oliver was cheating. She silently brooded, trying to think of some scheme to get even.

"Daddy and I have to be going soon, darling," her mother declared, with an apologetic smile. "Best we start gathering up our things and be on our way. Spencer, you be nice to Oliver, now; do you hear me?"

The girl replied with a nod, turning her head to conceal the scowl of displeasure on her face.

THE FOLLOWING MORNING, RAIN DICTATED THE CHILDREN'S schedule. Having to remain indoors, Oliver amused himself by playing a video game. Spencer had been invited to join him. Choosing to be antisocial, she refused, electing to read a book instead, still pouting over loosing at cards.

Oliver decided to try a ploy to get her to talk to him. "Do you want me to show you something that's a complete mystery?" he asked.

Spencer looked up, brushing the sides of her long auburn hair behind her ears. "Like what?" she replied skeptically.

The lad put down his video game controller and went to the mantelpiece. He opened the jewelry box and withdrew the key. "Here; look for yourself. "

The girl held the key in her hand, turning it over. "There's a silver coin in the middle. Where did they come from?"

"I don't know," Oliver replied. "The key was left here as a gift. We don't know who sent, though. Mom wore it around her neck for a while, but put it back in the box after deciding it was too heavy."

The girl examined both sides of the object closely.

"Spencer, what are you doing? Stop tapping the key on the flat of your hand," Oliver demanded. "You might break it."

"It looks as though the coin is jammed in the embossed circle. If I can get it out, we can take a closer look and find a clue." Spencer tapped again. "Yes; I was right," she declared as the coin fell into her palm.

"Let me have it," Oliver demanded.

"Not so fast. I'm the one who got it out." The girl swiveled so that her back was to the boy and turned the coin over. "Numbers. 1 9 0 2 and 1 9 5 2. It's code."

"No, it's not. They're dates, silly. Nineteen-oh-two and nineteen-fifty-two."

"If you say so." Spencer turned the coin over. "How about these then? It says *2.5 c* and *900 m*. Definitely code."

"Let me look." Oliver made a grab for the coin but succeeded only in knocking it out of Spencer's hand.

After hitting the ground, it rolled across the floor and under the piano. Oliver knelt to look. "Can't see it," he informed Spencer, before laying outstretched to gain a better view. "Still can't see it."

"Get up, Olly, before your mom comes in, and you have to explain you've lost the coin."

"Me? I'm not the one who took it out of the key. It's all your fault."

"Don't worry, Olly. It can't have rolled far. We'll look for it later. Put the key back in the box, and I'll play you at speed racing if you like."

Julia and Cordelia were in the kitchen, baking. Shadow sat under the table, hoping for crumbs to fall on the floor. However, when the dog ventured near the stove, he was banished, being told to go and find the children.

A minute later, the Spaniel came into the parlor, a rubber ball in its mouth.

"You found your toy," Spencer declared, putting down her

gaming controller. "Clever boy. Do you want to play?" The dog dropped the ball at her feet.

The girl bounced the ball on the floor, and Shadow caught it in his mouth straight away. The dog then dropped the ball in front of Oliver.

"Your turn, Olly. Bounce it nice and high," Spencer told him.

"Okay. Ready?"

Shadow barked enthusiastically.

With all his might, Oliver threw the ball down. It rebounded so high it almost touched the ceiling. Too fast for the dog, Shadow waited for the second bounce and then launched himself into the air. Hopelessly mistiming the movement, he managed to knock the ball upwards and sideways.

Thwack! The ball hit the lower corner of the painting, which hung to the side of the fireplace.

"Oh my goodness," Spencer exclaimed. "I hope we haven't damaged the frame."

"Nah," Oliver casually replied after inspecting the artwork. "I just need to straighten it up, that's all." After a slight adjustment, he stepped back. "There. Good as new. Mom will never know."

Spencer moved closer to look for herself. "We're lucky, I guess. What's this note on the floor? It wasn't here a moment ago." Shadow pushed his way forward, seizing the paper before either child could stop him.

The dog darted away, pausing on the far side of the coffee table. Oliver moved towards the animal.

Shadow waited until the boy was only an arm's length away and shot around to the other side. Oliver tried again. The dog repeated the maneuver, leaving Oliver still a coffee-table distance away.

"Keep still, Olly. Shadow thinks it's a game. The more you chase him, the more he'll run around the table."

The boy stopped. The dog stretched out on the floor and dropped the paper.

"Don't move, Olly. Shadow will be quicker than you if you do." Then addressing the dog, Spencer commanded, "Shadow, come. Good boy. Drop it."

"Wow; that's incredible. How did you manage that?" Oliver asked, as Spencer triumphantly held up the gently chewed paper.

"Practice and lots of doggie treats. Watch out your mom doesn't decide to train you the same way." The girl laughed at the joke as she inspected the sheet.

"It is damaged?" Oliver inquired.

"A smidgen, on one edge, although you'd hardly notice."

"Any of the writing missing?"

"Hard to tell," Spencer replied. "Probably not important."

"Let me see," Oliver asked, holding out a hand. "I've seen that type of diagram before, inside packets of pills, together with lots of other information."

"You're right, Olly. It's a chemical formula. I wonder what it stands for."

"You two are very quiet," Julia observed carry glasses of lemonade, on a tray, into the parlor. "What are you up to?"

"Not much, Mom," was the lad's reflex reply.

"Sure doesn't look like *not much*. Show me."

Reluctantly, Oliver handed over the paper. "It dropped from behind one of the paintings. It's a formula. Spencer and I are trying to figure out what it means by using the computer."

"Any luck?" his mother asked.

"Not so far," Aunt Julia. "We can't find a picture anywhere that matches."

"Maybe I can help?" After studying the diagram for a minute, Julia told Spencer to *Google* LSD.

The girl read aloud the first result.

"A synthetic crystalline compound, lysergic acid die-thy-lamide, that is a potent halluc-in-ogenic drug."

"Now see if you can find the 2D structural formula. Click on *Wikipedia*."

A moment later, up came the image.

"I thought so," Julia continued. "See, here and here, there's a close match. Now search for *Magic Mushroom.*"

Wikipedia redirected to 'Psilocybin mushroom.' Spencer read the opening text, as before, stumbling over unfamiliar words.

"A psilo-cybin mushroom is one of a poly-phy-letic group of fungi that contain any of various psych-edelic compounds, including psil-o-cybin, psil-o-cin, and bae-ocystin."

"What are *psychedelic compounds*?" Oliver asked.

"They are drugs that can expand people's awareness; open up their minds if you like," his mother replied. "From what I can remember reading when I worked as a nurse, there can be serious side effects. Dangerous stuff, in the wrong hands. Scroll down to the formulae structures." Spencer did as she was directed. "Look. There are other matches, here and here." Julia pointed. "I think this part depicts Rohypnol, which is a very potent tranquilizer. Sometimes proscribed as a sleeping pill, if misused, it has a paralyzing effect. In high doses, it can kill a person. I wonder who would want to create this concoction and why?"

There was a polite coughing sound. "Excuse me. I don't want to break up the party but anyone ready for a slice of cake?"

"Me." "Me." The children responded almost in unison to Cordelia's invitation, leaving Julia's question unanswered and ultimately forgotten.

50

"I'VE BEEN IN TOUCH WITH SEONG-HO, AND INVITED HIM BACK TO the island, although it's going be a week or so before he arrives," Harper told Federico and Karmina.

"Why so long?" the Brazilian asked. "Last time he was here in no time at all."

"I gave him a shopping list of things I want him to bring over here; things not easily obtained in Cuba."

"Contraband, you mean?" Federico responded. "Good god, *cúmbila* [pal]; what are we getting into?"

"Ask me no questions, and I'll tell you no lies," the American answered with a smirk. "This evening, we have nowhere to go in particular. Do either of you have any suggestions?"

"Actually, I do. There's a parade in the old quarter," Karmina informed them. "Lots of music, dancing, and good food. Hands up, who's coming with me?"

The crowd of people parted as the procession made its way diagonally across the plaza. The participants were dressed in brightly-colored costumes as they passed by, while the onlookers clapped in time with the lively music. Everyone was having a good time.

"What are they celebrating?" Harper asked.

"Watch, enjoy the spectacle, and you will find out," Federico responded.

A choir followed, singing an uplifting hymn, reminding Harper of the time he had attended a religious festival when he was a boy. Behind the singers walked rows of children aged between five and fifteen. All were dressed in white, their faces covered in masks. Each mask depicted a slightly different expression of happiness, focusing around oversized thick-lipped smiles and rosy cheeks. In the middle, carried aloft, was an effigy of a saint. Dressed in bright robes, he had wings carved out of alabaster.

"The sculpture represents the Guardian Angel," Federico shouted over the noise. "He's protecting the children from harm."

"Is that why they are so happy? They are singing about *Santo Ángel Custodio?*"

"You've got it, Harper. Your Spanish is improving."

A couple of minutes later, another troop could be heard approaching. The accompany music sounded like the dirge expected during a funeral procession. When in view, the majority of participants had bedsheets, dyed in shades of dark grey, draped over their heads. Their faces, too, were masked. This time, the images were themed on a skeleton's skull.

This group was accompanied by men wearing dark crimson cloaks with black hoods that hid their features. They carried firebrands and were the ones chanting that mournful lament.

"What are those two groups all about?" Harper inquired.

"The people in the center symbolize missing persons whose souls have been snatched away by *El Coco*. Those carrying torches represent the evil spirit's followers."

"*El Coco,*" the American repeated. "I've heard that name before."

"Everyone in Cuba is afraid of *El Coco*, the bogeyman, Harper."

51

"Waaaaahh."

Oliver opened his eyes to see a figure, head covered with a white sheet, standing beside his bed. "You didn't fool me, Spencer. I know it's you. Who are you supposed to be?"

The girl pulled the sheet off her head, pressed her face close to Oliver's, and leered, wide-eyed. "The bogeyman, of course."

"You don't look like the bogeyman. For starters, your bedsheet's the wrong color, and no self-respecting ghost wears Harry Potty glasses."

"Leave my spectacles out of this, Oliver Harper. You think you're so clever, don't you?" Spencer pulled back, brushing her auburn hair out of her eyes. "Just because you won at cards."

"That is because I'm super smart. I was born that way you know."

"Oh yeah. If you are so intelligent, what's the longest word in the English dictionary?"

After sitting up in bed, the boy replied with a grin, "Antidisestablishmentarianism. My dad taught me that."

"Wrong!" Spencer intoned, her voice resonating as if a tenor bell had been struck. "The longest word is *smiles*."

"Nonsense," Oliver responded. After counting on his fingers, he continued. "*Smiles* has only six letters."

Shadow, who had jumped onto Oliver's bed, suddenly became alert, his, ears pricked up

"Six letters, yes, but it has a *mile* between the two *esses*. Ha, ha; got yah."

Interrupting the banter, the Spaniel started a low guttural growl.

"What is it, Shadow; what's got you so spooked?" Spencer asked.

"Probably the bogeyman." Oliver chuckled.

A clomping noise echoed up from the room below.

"With big feet. I don't think so. We should go take a look," Spencer suggested. "Unless Mr. Know-it-all is too scared."

"I'm not scared," Oliver answered by way of a rebuttal, as he got out of bed. "It's probably Miss Cordelia."

"In that case, bring your top sheet. Together, we can give our great-aunt the fright of her life. Shadow, you stay here and be quiet. We don't want you giving the game away."

"There's no light on in the parlor," Oliver whispered when the pair reached the bottom of the stairs.

"Probably a fuse," Spencer suggested. "I expect Cordelia is trying to fix it. Anyway, all the better if we are going to play ghosts. Are you ready? On three. One, two, three."

"Booo!" The two children jumped into the parlor doorway, heads covered by the sheets.

A flashlight shone in their direction.

"Well looky here, Midnight. A couple of zombies ready to convert us into walking dead." The speaker could have been a ghoul himself, his face and hands covered in the scars from second and third-degree burns.

A second man stepped forward and pulled the sheets off the children's heads. "You must be Oliver," he said. "And you, young lady, I'd don't believe I've had the pleasure."

"What are you two doing here?" the boy asked. "I'm going to call my mom."

"You do that, lad," Scarface responded. "She knows who we are. We've come to say hello."

"Mom! Mom, come downstairs quick," Oliver shouted. "There are some people here who want to speak to you."

Julia was awakened by the sound of her son calling. Half asleep, she pulled on her dressing gown. Oliver called for a second time. Hurriedly she made her way across the landing, descended the stairs, and walked into the front parlor.

She looked in astonishment at the two men. Slowly her brain put names to faces, although it took a little longer for the scarred man.

"Mitchell, what are you doing here? And Conrad White; you're supposed to be dead."

"Do I look dead?" White replied, his heavily pockmarked face contorting into an even more menacing appearance. "No thanks to your husband, I might say. The submarine torpedoing the command center of the ocean prison killed everyone except me. I have a score to settle with Roger Harper when we meet up. As for you, no doubt you put him up to it, you bitch."

"Now, now, Conrad. We didn't come here to hurl insults at the good lady. We require some information from her instead."

Julia's mind seethed in a turmoil of hatred. At the behest of Doctors Hyde and Daniels, Warden White had dragooned her into acting as medical orderly for the inmates he unlawfully imprisoned on the oil platforms in the Gulf of Mexico. She, too, had a score to settle but decided with the children present, now was not the time to invite a confrontation.

"You had a visitor a few days ago," Mitchell told her. "Why did he come here?"

"Who do you mean?"

"Seong-ho Moon," Mitchell replied. "You remember him, don't

you? A short guy, who walks with a limp on account of a busted kneecap. He helped you and Harper escape. Why was the Korean here?"

"You are mistaken. I haven't seen him."

"Then why are you so nervous?" was Mitchell's next question.

"Wouldn't you be, after two strangers barge in here unannounced?"

"We're hardly strangers. Tell us what you know, and the kids will come to no harm. Isn't that right, Conrad?"

"Leave them out of this, Midnight." Julia endeavored to sound assertive, trying to ignore the rapid increase of her heartbeat. "Children, go back upstairs."

Oliver and Spencer made to leave. "Not so fast, young'uns." White moved to grab the pair but only succeeded in seizing the boy. Spencer slipped to the side and stood behind Julia.

"Let me go. You're hurting me," Oliver squealed, wriggling madly in the Warden's clutches.

"Keep still, you little tyke, or I really will hurt you."

"Leave him alone," Julia pleaded, "and I'll tell you what you want to know." White loosened his grip a little. "You'll find a key inside the leather-covered jewelry box on the mantelpiece. I don't know who left it."

Mitchell went over to the fireplace. After picking up the box, opening the lid, and taking out the key, he let it dangle by the gold chain. "Well, I never. Doctor Daniels will be pleased."

"You know what it's for?" asked Julia.

"Yes indeedy, but that's none of your concern," Mitchell answered, placing the key inside his coat pocket.

"You have the key. Now go before I call the police."

White chuckled. "Really? I don't think we can allow that." Oliver squirmed some more, kicking a chair over as he struggled. "Ouch, you little bugger. You've just bit me."

"Let the boy go," Mitchell ordered. "We have the key. Let's get out of here."

As soon as Oliver was free, he rushed to stand next to Spencer. The two men moved into the hallway. "At least they didn't take the formula," the boy whispered in the girl's ear, be it a little too loudly.

Mitchell swiveled on his heels. "Formula; what formula? I swear I'll let Conrad break every bone in your son's body if you don't tell me, Julia Harper."

"Next door, in the left-hand drawer of the sideboard, you'll find a folded piece of paper. It contains a formula of some kind. The children found it tucked behind one of the pictures on the fireplace wall."

"Okay, lead the way," Mitchell commanded. "Conrad, you bring up the rear and make sure there's no funny business from these two brats."

Upon opening the drawer, Mitchell lifted out the paper and opened it out. "Mmm. I've no idea what this means. How about you, Conrad?"

The Warden took a glance. "Same here. You and I may not understand it, but Doctor Daniels certainly will. He'll be well pleased when we bring it to him."

"Don't either of you two men move," an authoritative voice commanded for the hallway. Cordelia was standing there, pointing the 21-inch barrel of a squirrel gun at White's chest. "Children, go into the kitchen. One of you dial 911. Hurry."

Oliver and Spencer left.

"Put that piece of paper down, right now, or I'll shoot your companion."

"Surely not. Miss Julia and I go back a long way. We're practically BFFs, aren't we Jules?" Mitchell smirked at using her husband's term of endearment, as he slowly placed the paper on the sideboard with an exaggerated movement.

For only a second, Cordelia's eyes wondered to the formula, but long enough for White to reach for the handgun tucked into his waistband.

Blamb!

The sound was earsplitting. Julia turned towards her aunt, and then to the Warden. She saw a red stain on the man's chest. A second later, Conrad White crumpled onto the floor.

"Nice shooting if I may say so." Mitchell took a moment to check the Warden's pulse. "Dead as a doornail. Twice the reward for me." He picked up the paper and moved towards the exit.

"Take another step, and you'll join your playmate in kingdom come."

"Are you sure about that?" Mitchell asked. "If I'm not mistaken, what you are holding is a Savage .22 single-shot rifle." He gave a knowing smile. "As a kid, my daddy used to take me hunting. I know my guns. Go on, pull the trigger for all the good it will do you."

Cordelia cursed in a most unladylike manner, stepping aside as Mitchell pushed his way into the hall.

"Everyone take care now. Miss me lots," Kirt Mitchell remarked, as he opened the front door. "I'll say hi to Roger, from you all, next time we bump into each other."

"Roger's alive? The government told me he is dead. I've his ashes to prove it."

If Julia expected an answer, she was mistaken. Mitchell was hurrying down the garden path, anxious to be well clear of the premises before the police arrived.

"Are you going to tell him?" Aunt Cordelia asked Julia as they sat on the bed in one of the spare bedrooms of the house next door. Oliver, Spencer, and the dog were asleep in the adjacent room. With their own house still the center of a police investigation of a home invasion, they thought it best to stay elsewhere, at least for the rest of the night.

"I think not," Julia replied, annunciating her words slowly. "That weasel, Midnight, could never be trusted to tell the truth. I don't want to get Olly's hopes up, only to have them dashed later."

"But you believe Roger is alive, don't you, Julia?" Cordelia clasped her hands around her niece's. "I can tell by the look on your face."

"Yes, Aunty, I do." The words came between sobs of joy.

CROSSING THE US/MEXICAN BORDER AT *LAREDO* HAD BEEN trouble-free, as had the earlier, be it tiring, drive from California, through Arizona to Texas.

Dr. Peter Lee, a marine biologist, he had told the border guards, showing a passport, driver's license, and vehicle registration to support his assumed identity. Fieldwork in *Laguna de Términos*, studying mollusks, he had informed them. A total fabrication, but nobody questioned his story.

From the border crossing, he continued south along *85* and then *83*. Reaching *Veracruz*, he stopped to change the vehicle's plates for those off of a Mexican car. He did not want people to think he was an American tourist and an easy mark of a robbery or an abduction.

He turned east, following the coast road, driving past his declared destination. Continuing until he came to the small fishing village of *Puerto Cancún*, there he found a rickety dock made of wood pylons and nailed boards. The journey had covered just under three thousand miles. Discounting breaks and overnight stops, he had been sixty-seven hours at the wheel. Two men were awaiting his arrival.

"*Señor* Lee, I am so glad you could make it. The equipment you requested is already loaded onto the fishing boat." The speaker, wearing an out of place business suit, smiled and held out a hand. After the briefest of handshakes, the leader of the local drug cartel continued, "and this is *su capitán*. He will take good care of you from here on."

El capitán swayed nervously from foot to foot, anxious to be out of the presence of *Mejor Amiga* [Best Friend], as the drug lord liked to be known.

"Give me my payment, and I will be on my way."

Lee handed over a small satchel containing twenty thousand American dollars. After a cursory look, *Mejor Amiga* departed, delighted, that for little effort on his part, he had made so much money.

The captain looked relieved, indicating they should be on their way. The journey of four hundred and fifty miles would take all of fifty-six hours.

I hope this is not a waste of my time, Seong-ho thought to himself as they left the dock. Ten days ago, he had been sitting in his office, writing code for a piece of firewall software when Harper's email requested, once more, the Korean's assistance in Cuba.

What with the continual pitch and yore of the vessel, Seong-ho had gotten little sleep, laying on the bunk in the small cabin. Finally, having decided to join the captain, he stood behind the glass of the wheelhouse, gripping the railing so hard his knuckles turned white. The Korean silently prayed that the flickering lights ahead were coming from the island and not a patrol boat.

For the moment, looking down at his right hand, he reflected on the signet ring worn on his pinkie finger. A present from his father for his twenty-first birthday, the motif was that of a 17th-century sailing vessel. Seong-ho recalled, after opening the gift, contemplating the engraved inscription on the inside: FAITH • CHARITY. At the time, his father has said, "*Have faith in yourself son and be charitable to others.*" That had been his motto ever since.

"The signet ring." He voiced the words, remembering his stay at the *Indigo Hotel* in Savannah. The Korean had walked up to the concierge's desk and asked if he had any paper to wrap a small gift.

"Of course, sir." was the courteous reply. "If you have it with you, I would be more than happy to do the honors." Seong-ho produced the corn-colored leather jewelry box. "For a lady, I presume?" The Korean nodded in reply.

The concierge rummaged under the counter and produced a variety of wrapping papers. Ignoring the bright selection of colors, Seong-ho chose plain brown parcel paper. Without comment, the box was quickly wrapped. From a drawer, the concierge removed a stick of sealing wax. "Adds a touch of class. Much better than common sticky-tape, don't you think, sir?" After lighting a match, a blob of wax dripped onto the flap.

"What are you doing?" Seong-ho hurriedly asked as the man was about to emboss the soft wax with the hotel's seal. "Stop! I would prefer you to use this instead." That is when the Korean slipped the ring off his finger and handed over.

Cresting a colossal wave, the bow of the fishing boat lifted violently before slamming down hard, bring the Korean back to the present. Once more, Seong-ho gripped the railing. *I wonder if Julia noticed the sailing vessel seal? If she did, she probably didn't realize it is from my ring. Poor Julia. I can't imagine what you're going through. I wish I could have told you that your husband is alive.*

The vessel suddenly changed direction, veering to starboard, which caused the Korean to fear he was about to become the victim of some kind of double-cross.

53

THE BOAT'S CAPTAIN SAW THE LOOK OF PANIC ON SEONG-HO'S FACE. "Relax, *señor* Lee," the Korean was told, as nets were tossed over the side. "Nobody will think anything of it if they see us fishing. In half an hour, we'll tack the other way. You and your precious cargo will be ashore before daylight."

Fifty yards from the beach, the sea anchor dropped. The captain hauled in the line that had been towing a small dinghy behind them. After being securely tied to the side of the boat, the Korean climbed into it.

Packages were flung from the fishing vessel to the dinghy, which Seong-ho deftly caught and stowed away. Next, the captain started the winch that, with the use of the boat's gantry, would lift the heaviest item and lower it over the side of the vessel.

The motorcycle bobbed up and down, with attached floats keeping it out of the water. In short order, the two men headed for the shore, beached the motorcycle, and hastily offloaded the packages.

Without offering further help, the captain rowed back to the fishing boat, and within minutes he was heading back to Mexico. Seong-ho could see the man standing on the deck waving, a big smile on his face. And why not? In his other hand, he held a bundle of one hundred dollar bills totaling $10,000.

After carefully stashing the equipment into the motorcycle's panniers or his backpack, the Korean was ready to leave. Before doing so however, Seong-ho switched on the battery-operated device, which provided a satellite Wi-Fi hotspot connection for his smartphone. He wrote a three-word email and sent it to Harper.

THE EAGLE HAS LANDED

To the uninitiated, it meant nothing. Some may have thought it was a reference to the Armstrong/Aldrin module of Apollo 11's mission. To Harper, it indicated that Seong-ho *Moon* had returned safely to the island.

DESPITE THE CONGENIAL SURROUNDINGS, KIRT MITCHELL FELT uncomfortable as he sat in the chair opposite Daniels. Situated in an underground room, the Doctor had spent the past five minutes examining the formula that Mitchell had 'acquired' during his trip to Savannah. From time to time, Daniels would make a short notation on a notepad.

Looking up, Daniels smiled. "You did well, Mitchell. This piece of paper could well be the solution to my quest. Most certainly, I shall be awarded a double Nobel Prize in Physics and Chemistry, going down in history to be the most renowned scientist ever. Pity about Conrad White. I was thinking of appointing him director of a new research facility in Argentina that I am sponsoring." In response to Mitchell's incredulous look, the Doctor gave a thin smile. "Well, not exactly a director, but you know what I mean. Before you left, I trust you made sure he was dead?"

Mitchell nodded his head slowly.

"Good. We don't want any loose ends." Using the key that Mitchell had earlier given him, Daniels tapped the notepad to add emphasis to his next question. "You took this very key to the museum, and with it were able to look inside the bookcase drawer in Batista's office?"

"Yes, Doctor. I succeeded in unlocking the drawer, but there was nothing there. I checked all the other drawers as well, including the desk. All were empty."

"You saw nothing like this elsewhere in the room?" Daniels opened his desk's drawer and pulled out a *diez centavos* [ten cents] coin. Mitchell, this time, shook his head. "Not set into the handle of a letter opener, for example?" the doctor elaborated.

"No, sir. I'm certain there wasn't. On Batista's desk were a leather-backed blotting-pad, a penholder with a fountain pen, and a gold telephone. Nothing else, as I recall."

"So, the coin has yet to arrive."

"Sorry, Doctor Daniels, I don't understand what you mean by *the coin has yet to arrive*."

"So far, I have not succeeded in teleporting a coin into the bookcase drawer," Daniels explained in a despondent tone.

Then he brightened up. "However, with this formula, after I have injected the test subjects, they will have enhanced cerebral capacity. It's only a matter of days, and I shall triumph." The Doctor went back to his notepad. Realizing Mitchell was not getting up to leave, he added, "That will be all for now. I'll let you know if I need your assistance again. Dismissed."

Mitchell remained seated, apprehensively biting his fingernails.

"I said dismissed."

"Sir, there's something else you should know."

"Well?" The Doctor was becoming irritable. "Speak your mind."

"At the *Museo de la Revolución*, as I was leaving, one of the curators remarked that previously another person had been inside Batista's private office, excluding the regular staff that is."

"Did this curator give you a name or description?"

"Apart from saying he was male, no. The curator seemed extraordinarily vague on that point. Couldn't tell me the man's height or hair color, for example. However, he did recall his Spanish was a little forced."

"Forced, how do you mean?" Daniels asked.

"As in spoken by a foreigner unsure of the language," Mitchell replied. "It has to be Harper. He would be able to mess with the curator's memory. I bet he retrieved the coin."

"*Vielleicht.* [Perhaps.] However, if he has, there was nothing for you to find. Now be on your way, Mitchell," Tapping the piece paper, the Doctor then smiled. "Nevertheless, finding this formula is very fortuitous. Go and find Hans. He'll reimburse your out-of-pocket expenses. There's a bonus for you as well. You've earned it."

Mitchell retreated along the corridor. About to turn the corner, he heard Daniels exclaiming, "Yes, Robin; we did it! *Vater* [Father] would be so proud."

"Who is Robin? And who is Vater?" Mitchell asked himself. "Don't know. Don't care. Just show me the money, Hans. Show me the money."

55

SEONG-HO HAD LANDED NEAR THE BEACH RESORT OF *PLAYA CARIBE*.
Devoid of tourists at this early hour, he started his motorcycle and
road a few yards until he reached the metalled road. Nearby, a giant
plastic replica of a crab beckoned, advertising a seafood restaurant.
Unfortunately, it was closed.

The Korean was hungry and needed to find somewhere to eat.
He headed north until he reached *La Boca*. There, the road turned
east, following the meandering *Rio Guaurabo*. Having covered six and
a half miles, he found himself in the center of the town of *Trinidad*.
As he made his way along *Calle Desengaño*, he came across a row of
restaurants. They, too, were closed. Apart from the low thrum of
Seong-ho's motorcycle, the streets were quiet and empty.

Then he heard the sound of a radio coming from a side street.
The Koran slowed as he passed. The owner of *Casa Giroud* was
sweeping the sidewalk, singing along with the music.

In faltering Spanish, Seong-ho asked if she was serving
breakfast. Once he was fed and watered, the Korean requested the
use of the guesthouse's electricity as he had a piece of equipment he
needed to recharge. An hour later, after paying the bill, which
included a generous tip, he was again on his way.

Using the small GPS unit attached to the handlebars, he picked up route *152* and headed north.

Soon Seong-ho was passing the lush nature reserve of *Parque Natural Topes de Collantes*, on his right. A honeypot for outdoor adventurers, it featured waterfalls, scenic views, and hiking trails. However, the Korean had no time for hiking. Although tired, he pressed on for another sixty miles, taking the mountain roads, only stopping when he reached the start of the track that led to the abandoned coastal buildings.

Seong-ho looked at his watch. By his best estimate, it would be at least another hour before Harper, Federico, and Karmina would reach him. Ample time to investigate the crash site of the tanker mentioned by Harper in his last email

He hid the motorcycle in a small, disused quarry, covered it in brush, and set off down the slope. The toppled vehicle was easily spotted, the sun's rays reflecting off the stainless steel of the tanker's bodywork. The Korean took a moment to look towards the distant shoreline and wondered why a big rig would be going in that direction. With the coastal mist still needing the heat of the day to burn away, he found no answer.

Deciding the tanker itself might reveal a clue, carefully he placed each step as he negotiated the steep gradient. Now was not the time to fall and break a leg.

The tractor's cab was the first place Seong-ho looked. No sign of a body. Obviously, someone had removed it. There was a pair of sunglasses on the floor, one lens cracked. He looked for documentation, such as a work order, under the dashboard. There was none. Neither was the vehicle's title or registration, tucked behind one of the sun visors.

Climbing down, the Korean walked to the tanker itself. He rapped the sides. A dull thump near the bottom indicated there was still liquid inside.

Seong-ho clambered up the hillside for a few feet until he could obtain a bird's-eye view of the scene. It had rained since the crash, and a large number of bootprints were evident. He could see two sets leading back to the road. *Maybe that was the route taken when they recovered the body?*

Nothing more to be seen here, the Korean concluded. About to retrace his steps, he spotted something flapping in the wind. It took only a few seconds to walk over. There lay a piece of paper, with one corner stomped into the ground. Using a penknife, Seong-ho carefully freed it from the dried mud. Flattening the scrap out, he could see it was the remnant of a timesheet, with places of departure and arrival.

Something to tell Harper when he arrives, Seong-ho decided, for one phrase, in particular, stood out:

Planta Nuclear de Juraguá.

56

Again Kirt Mitchell was summoned, this time to the inner sanctum, deep underground, the location of Doctor Daniels' laboratories. He had never been there before, and other workers rarely spoke about the place, except to describe the ever-prevailing smell of chemicals. Hans, who was accompanying him, turned down a corridor that took them to a door labeled in three languages:

Área Restringida
Solo Personal Autorizado

Sperrgebiet
Nur Autorisiertes Personal

Restricted Area
Authorized Personnel Only

They went into a changing room.

"Pull the lab smock over your clothing. Take off your shoes and put on those clogs" the German-speaking Argentinian instructed.

As the two men dressed, Hans asked with a disdainful sneer, "Are you squeamish?"

"Why; what's in there?" Mitchell inquired, apprehensively. "I won't be exposed to some virus, will I?"

"Don't sound so nervous. The room is vacuum-sealed, and the air is filtered. We are safer in there than if we were in an isolation room at a hospital for highly contagious diseases."

Jesus. I must be crazy. Giving Harper up to Daniels and his brother was one thing, but this?

"Once inside, take deep breaths and try not to think about what you ate for breakfast. Otherwise, you will puke it all over your gown."

Thanks for the advice, buddy, Mitchell thought to himself.

The Argentinian was delighting in the lead-up to what was about to happen.

"Come on, Cinderella. Finish putting on your gown, or you'll be late for the ball." Hans laughed as he donned a shower cap. "Do you like my tiara?"

"Not really." Already Mitchell was feeling nauseous, and they were still in the changing room.

"That's too bad. You are required to wear one as well."

———————

Doctor Daniels was cursing at two orderlies who were struggling to remove a body from a circular vat. Similar to a swimming pool, the entire tank was lit from the sides. Three other bodies remained, floating on the surface, one still twitching. Thin electric cables, connected to skullcaps, snaked to separate control panels set around the perimeter.

Daniels shouted across the room, "Günter, as soon as this mess is cleaned away, have your team select four more specimens and get them wired up immediately. I want them acclimated as soon as possible."

"Yes, *Doktor*," was the reply. "Do you want to change the water first?" the question prompted by thin strands of blood meandering lazily back and forth across the surface.

"Good thinking. I don't want any contamination. See to it."

Günter snapped his heels together. "*Jawohl, Doktor.*" All that was lacking was the Nazi salute.

Hans coughed politely, which caused Daniels to turn around.

"Ah, Mitchell. Glad you could make it. You remember the formula you gave me?"

"Of course, sir?"

"How did you find it?" Daniels asked.

"I overheard Oliver, that's Harper's son, whispering to some girl that was with him. The mother gave it up after I threatened to break every bone in the boy's body."

The Doctor looked at Mitchell's minder and grinned. "Did you hear that, Hans. If you're not careful, our friend, here, will have your job."

From the response on Hans' face, he plainly did not consider the remark funny.

"Did the boy say anything else?" Daniels continued.

"No, sir," Mitchell answered. "Why do you ask?"

Daniels went to a stainless steel table nearby, returning with the formula encased in a plastic sleeve. "Mitchell, hold the paper up to the light. Does anything strike you as odd?"

After inspecting the contents, Kirt Mitchell replied, "Not really. Unless you are referring to the marks on one edge."

"Precisely, Mitchell. Precisely. Was there a dog in the house?"

"I did see one, if that's what you mean. Why do you ask?"

"Because those marks are made by a dog's teeth. If you'd looked more closely at the paper when you were in Savannah, you'd have realized part of the formula is missing."

"I'm no scientist, Doctor Daniels. I would not have known what to look for."

"Excuses. Excuses. Nothing but excuses." Daniels threw his hands up in exasperation.

"The children may not have seen the paper before the dog got hold of it," Mitchell volunteered, in self-defense.

"Nevertheless, if they had, you missed an opportunity to question them further. Now, I have to work out the missing symbols for myself." Daniels stormed back to the table and threw the formula down. "Lord knows how long it will take."

The orderlies had uncoupled the third body from the wiring and began lifting it from the vat, slopping water everywhere.

"Careful, you *Dummkopfe* [dunderheads]," Daniels growled. "Mind my clothing." As the orderlies muttered their apologies, he turned back to Mitchell. "Get out of my sight. Any more screwups on your part and I'll happily float you in this vat of porridge. Then I will have you wired you up to the machine and fry your brain. How would you like that, *mein Freund* [my friend]?"

THE SOUND OF TIRES CRUNCHING GRAVEL ANNOUNCED THE ARRIVAL of the Chevrolet Bel Air, rousing the Korean from his catnap. There were hugs and handshakes as he greeted the car's occupants.

"What are you looking so pleased about?" Harper asked, noticing the broad grin on Seong-ho's face, rather than the piece of paper he was holding in his right hand.

"Do you know what's down there?" the Korean asked, nodding in the direction of the coast.

"You do, I assume, so enlighten me," Harper responded.

"A nuclear power station."

"You've been doing some research in your spare time, I suppose?"

"Not on Google, if that's what you mean," Seong-ho replied. "While I was waiting for you, I checked out the wreckage. I found this."

Harper took the creased, mud-stained scrap of paper and looked at it. As the writing was in Spanish, he passed it over to Federico to translate.

"It's the tanker driver's log. Some entries refer to *planta nuclear.*

My goodness, I've just realized, that's the Juraguá nuclear facility we're talking about."

It took a moment of realization before Federico began to wring his hands together in despair. "Deus me ajude [God help me]!" the Brazilian exclaimed, in Portuguese. "I am a dead man."

"Whatever is the matter, Federico?" Harper asked, noting his friend's reaction.

"I drunk water from the nuclear plant. Heavy water. I am radioactive. I shall never see my homeland again."

"Easy, Federico, easy," Harper reassured him.

The Korean stood to the side, laughing.

"It's not funny, Seong-ho. Do something."

"Like what? I thought you were a journalist, Federico, and you'd have read up on such things. Heavy water, if that's what it is, is not radioactive."

"How should I know? I write copy for newspapers, not *Scientific American.*"

Harper began laughing too, as did Karmina.

"Come on, let's get started," the American suggested. "Did you bring the equipment I requested, Seong-ho?"

"Most of it," the Korean replied.

"What do you mean, most of it?" Harper began opening the panniers. "Where are the rifles?"

"We may be friends, Harper, but I am not risking a lifetime in a Cuban prison convicted of gun-running."

"Then how are we to take on the bad guys?" the American asked.

"Assuming there are bad guys, I have the very solution." Seong-ho dug into the bottom of the other side-pannier. "Needs a little assembly, that's all. Instructions not provided."

From the cover of the tropical vegetation, Harper began a slow commando crawl towards the cracked overgrown paving of the forecourt. A cluster of long-horned cattle, standing in the shade of a tree, looked lazily on as he made his final approach. Karmina, who had insisted she be more than a cultural adviser, was right beside him with the second crossbow. The American loaded a tranquilizer dart into his weapon. The Cuban did the same.

Now they waited.

Five minutes passed. The guard came sauntering along, following the line of the wall. He was tall, dark-skinned, and wore a crisp, official uniform not dissimilar to those worn by the Cuban police. Carrying no firearm that Harper could see, he wielded a baseball bat.

The guard stopped and turned. About to begin his walk back to the door, there was a twanging sound, followed by the noise of a man collapsing to the ground.

"Nice shot, Harper," Karmina declared, giving him the thumbs up. "I couldn't have done better myself. Shall we take out the other guard?"

Before Harper could answer, there was movement on a terrace, high up and behind the blockhouse. He sprang to his feet and set off in that direction, without a word of explanation. The Cuban woman was left to gather up the weapons and follow as best she could.

A young boy was standing a few yards away, as Harper crested the first terrace. Seeing the American, the lad scampered ahead, jumping onto the next terrace and then running towards a ventilation grill set into the far wall.

By the time Karmina caught up, Harper was standing next to the grill, bending over, hands on knees, trying to regain his breath.

"Whatever were you chasing, Harper?"

"I saw a young boy, about eight or nine years old," Harper answered. "He ran to this very spot. Now he's disappeared."

"I saw nobody," Karmina responded. "Are you sure it's not your imagination, Harper? Maybe you've got too much sun?"

"I saw him, I tell you. He looked just like the boy in my dream." The words spilled out of Harper's mouth. As soon as they did, he realized how ridiculous he sounded

Karmina shook her head but then stopped after noticing the grill had been removed and then put back in a hurry. She stepped forward and pulled on the mesh. The panel came away in her hand.

Harper stooped down. "What did I tell you? Someone has crawled through here. I can see scuff marks. We should see where this shaft leads."

"Is that wise, Harper? Best we go tell the others first."

"Nonsense. You'll be perfectly safe, I promise. However, leave the crossbows outside. It looks like we're in for a tight squeeze."

"Harper, wait," Karmina cautioned, but the American was already inside the opening. "This is not a good idea," she protested to the soles of his boots.

––––––––

Having traveled forty feet, the American concluded, "It's extremely dark in here. Did you bring a flashlight, Karmina?"

"What? I cannot hear you."

"A flashlight? Did you bring a flashlight?"

Finally catching up, she spoke from behind, "There's no need to shout, and no, I didn't."

"How about a lighter, then?"

"No. I don't smoke. We should go back."

"Federico has a lighter. He took it from a prison guard and forgot to return it."

"In case you haven't noticed, Harper, I am not Federico."

The American was not listening, having decided to grope his way towards the glimmer of light in the distance.

After another thirty feet or so, Harper stopped. At the end of the air duct, he found a vast circular chamber, the sides made from poured concrete. Daylight filtered in through displaced sheeting that was the roof, allowing him to see it housed a large tank covered in translucent material. *Plastic*, he thought. *There's a ladder on the far side. It shouldn't be too difficult to cross over and climb down.* "This way," he shouted over his shoulder.

Karmina watched as Harper proceeded. Once the American reached the center, he turned and indicated that she should follow.

After stepping gingerly onto the cover, the Cuban felt it give slightly. Deciding on a more prudent approach, she took the longer route around the circumference.

"I'm almost there," Harper called, not looking back. "Are you …"

Whatever the end of Harper's question might have been, the words were lost under the loud splintering sound of the covering beginning to rupture. Small lines at first, radiating from where the American knelt. More cracks quickly followed. The tank's cover began to sag alarmingly. Shards of plastic exploded downward, as the central pieces shattered. Within seconds Harper was falling.

Karmina congratulated herself that she had chosen to remain near the edge. However, an earsplitting sound resonated up to the ceiling, as the whole of the dome caved in. Her scream echoed around the chamber, as she, too, tumbled into the void.

FEDERICO WATCHED SEONG-HO UNBOX THE DRONE BROUGHT FROM Mexico. "So this is why you snuck in under the radar," he said with a smile. "Harper should have told me, and I would have said he needn't have bothered. For a price, such things can be obtained here on the island."

"The fewer people that know what we are doing, the better," the Korean replied.

"Oh, yeah. Harper didn't think so this morning before we left. He had me call my press office and tell them I was investigation strange going on around here. He said a little publicity might rattle a few cages. He wants to see if anyone panics."

"Did you mention this location, Federico?"

"I told them where the road tanker had crashed," Federico responded.

"And your press office; were they interested?"

"Not really. A motor vehicle accident is hardly front-page news." The Brazilian turned towards Harper and Karmina, who were standing twenty feet away, trying to assemble the parts Seong-ho had given then. "How's it going over there?" he shouted.

Harper walked over, holding two pieces that looked the same.

Karmina joined him. She was clutching another part that was long and flat.

"If I knew what this is supposed to be, it would help."

"Don't look at me," Federico responded. "I'm just a hack journalist, remember?"

The Korean glanced up from the video monitor that was part of the drone's controller. "It's a crossbow. I'd have thought you would have figured that out for yourselves. What you are holding, Harper, are the left and right bow limbs. They should snap together, tighter than a bug in a rug.

"Karmina, that's a section of the barrel," Seong-ho told her. Pointing with his finger, he continued, "See this; it's the flight groove running down the center. Look for two similar sections. Other pieces you'll need to identify are the stock, cocking strip, retention spring, and trigger."

"You're loving watching me trying to figure it out, aren't you, Seong-ho?"

"Good practice when you return home, and Oliver needs your help assembling model aircraft and the like."

"And this crossbow is supposed to serve as a substitute for a rifle." Harper pulled a face as though someone had handed him a used diaper. "May I remind you, Seong-ho, that I'm a former army ranger, not a French archer at the Battle of *Crécy*. What's the distance this thing can accurately reach, anyway?"

"Thirty to thirty-five yards. Any further away and you'll probably miss,"

"So you chose a crossbow over a rifle that can be fired from half a mile away with pinpoint accuracy. Is that what I'm hearing?" Harper was more than a little upset.

"May I point out, the crossbow is virtually silent when fired; a rifle is not. And I've already told you, I was not going to risk a lifetime in jail, even for you, Harper." The Korean reached down into the backpack that was at his feet and removed two boxes. "Here's your ammunition."

Harper took the boxes and carefully opened one. He was looking at six small arrows. "Tranquilizing darts? What with an ineffective weapon, and now these. I'd be better off going up to the enemy and shaking their hand."

Seong-ho chuckled. "Or stabbing them in the neck with the tranquilizer. Your choice."

———

There were enough pieces to assemble two crossbows. The Korean flight tested the drone and then declared it was time to eat. "I hope you've brought something nice."

The others looked at each other.

"Did you put the packed lunches in the trunk of the car, Federico?" Karmina asked.

The Brazilian shook his head.

"How about you, Harper?"

"Damn. I knew we'd left something in the apartment."

"What? Don't tell me you've brought no food."

"Sorry, buddy," Harper replied. "D'you want me to go hunt some big game with a crossbow?"

"I don't believe it." The Korean's face turned red in exasperation. "I come all this way, and this is how I'm treated."

It was Harper's turn to chuckle. "Just kidding, my friend. Now you know how it feels to be frustrated. Next time you want something put together, give us a diagram of the end product or do it yourself."

———

Come two o'clock, the three men and the woman were standing on a small promontory overlooking the derelict nuclear plant. From there, they moved west, following the contour, increasing the distance between themselves and the access road. A hundred yards further, Harper decided to stop. There was a cluster of large boulders that would keep them hidden from the track and the facility itself if they crouched down.

Using binoculars, Federico saw no sign of movement on the

ground. A peregrine falcon glided lazily on the uplift of thermals, searching for prey. Seemingly, both man and bird were out of luck.

"Okay; over to you, Seong-ho," Harper instructed. "Get that drone into the air so that we can find out what's going on down there."

Federico pointed to a smudge on the monitor, at the same time whispering, "I think there's a man in the shadow of that tree."

"Can you zoom the camera in?" Harper asked the Korean.

"No problem," Seong-ho replied. "How's that?"

"It's a guard, all right," the American declared. "And when there's one, there will certainly be more. Keep searching, Seong-ho. Pan over to the right. We've not looked there."

A few minutes later, another guard was spotted by a door into another part of the facility.

"Shall we move in?" Federico asked.

"To be sure, allow Seong-ho to do one more sweep. I don't want any surprises," was Harper's answer.

"What the devil was that?" Karmina, who had been looking over the Koreans shoulder, asked as the drone's camera lurched suddenly to the left and then began tumbling towards the earth.

Seong-ho wrestled with the controls, bringing the drone under control and landing it on the ground. The camera, still functioning, picked up an angry falcon pecking at the lens.

"It seems the bird has mistaken our drone for lunch," the Korean observed. "And I think it has broken off one of the propellers. That puppy isn't going to fly anymore, not today anyway."

"So what do we do now?" was the Karmina's next question.

"We go and find out what's behind the door that guard is protecting," Harper told everyone. "Come on; follow me. And be quiet about it."

60

"YOU TWO CERTAINLY TOOK THE HARD WAY DOWN," SO SPOKE Seong-ho as he stood at the edge of the vat of water. "Are the pair of you enjoying your swim?"

"And hello to you too," Harper responded, spitting out a mouthful of liquid. "How did you get in here?"

"Federico and I walked through the front door. How's that for originality? We saw you and Karmina race off and disappear into a ventilation shaft. As civilized people, we don't use someone's swimming pool without asking."

"This is no swimming pool," Harper disputed, as he climbed out. After helping Karmina, he asked, "What's all that machinery over there?"

"I'll take a look," the Korean volunteered, "while you and Karmina drip-dry yourselves."

A couple of minutes later, Seong-ho returned. "At the far end is a pipe and a pump, designed to bring seawater into this place. Beside it, there's what looks to be a reverse osmosis unit used to desalinate the water. The machinery nearest to us, I'm not quite sure, but I'm thinking it's a commercial ionizer capable of processing hundreds of gallons per minute."

"So I have been swimming in ionized water," the Cuban woman proclaimed. "Great. I suppose now I will glow in the dark."

"No, Karmina, you won't," the Korean told her. "You're acting paranoid, like your boyfriend. Some people drink it, believing it's beneficial to their health. So stop worrying about glowing in the dark."

"It would be rather funny if you did, sweetheart," thought Federico. "You'd be assured a place in the next street parade."

"Enough banter. Seriously, Seong-ho, what other uses are there for thousands of gallons of ionized water?" the American asked.

"Let me think."

"It improves the electrical conductively of water," Federico proclaimed excitedly, interrupting the Korean's thought.

"He's right, Harper," Seong-ho agreed. "How did you know that?"

Francisco shrugged his shoulders. "I'm not sure. Maybe I read it in *Healthy Living Magazine*?"

Enthusiastically slapping the Brazilian on the back, Harper added, with a smile, "There's still hope for you, Federico. We'll make a scientist of you yet."

"Ouch! Not so hard." About to complain some more, Federico was interrupted by a sound. "What's that?" he asked. "It's coming from outside, I think."

"Only one way to find out," Harper told them. "Keep close to the wall and stay behind me."

Forming a column, everyone moved in unison until they reached the door. The American slowly pushed it ajar and peeked through the crack.

"What do you see?" the Brazilian whispered. "Anything?"

"Another road tanker has just driven up. The driver is getting out."

The commentary continued in a hushed tone, "He's talking to someone. It's the other guard. Now the driver is climbing a ladder on the side of the tanker."

Harper paused for a few seconds.

"He's on the roof and opening the loading hatch. Now, he's

putting a fill hose, that is suspended from a gantry, into the tank itself."

Another short break in the American's commentary.

"The driver is giving a thumbs-up sign."

The sound of an electric motor starting filtered through the doorway.

"The guard on the ground has just pushed a button on a panel. I think the tanker has started filling with water."

"We should go tackle them," Federico suggested. "The driver could tell us who he's working for."

"Assuming they talk," Seong-ho countered.

"I have a better idea," Karmina announced. "If we wait until the truck leaves and follow it, we'll find out where the driver is delivering his cargo."

"Good idea," the Korean concurred. "We had better start hoofing it right now. Otherwise, by the time we reach the vehicles, the tanker will be long gone. The last person to arrive at the quarry buys the first round of drinks this evening."

There was not much of the evening left by the time the quartet reached Havana. Taking turns, first the motorcycle and then the Chevrolet, they shadowed the road tanker.

Their plan was working well until they by-passed *Aguada de Pasajeros*. As the twenty-two wheeler approached the junction that would take it onto the *Autopista Nacional*, the main arterial route to Havana, it slowed and stopped at the rear of a line of traffic. Ahead was the strobing blue light of a police car.

Federico, who was driving the Chevrolet, pulled onto the shoulder. Seong-ho came up behind, stopped, and got off his motorcycle. Other vehicles drove past, stopping as they joined the queue.

"What shall we do now?" Federico asked. "Harper has no documents. *La policía* may arrest him."

"I could continue," the Korean suggested. "I have a passport and driver's license."

"And when they ask you what you're doing in Cuba?" was Federico's open question.

"I don't know, but I'm sure I think of something."

"Too risky."

"How do you mean, Harper,"

"Just like before, at the railway and bus station, they are looking for someone. Not me, though. My death has already hit the newscasts. I'm guessing you, Federico, are the focus of the manhunt.".

"You guys are jumping to conclusions. Hold on a second," Karmina told them as she exited the car.

"Where is she going?" Harper asked.

"*Sei lá* [Search me]," the Brazilian replied in his native tongue.

Karmina flagged down an oncoming truck. The driver leaned through the window. There was a brief, inaudible, conversation.

"Well?" the two men asked in unison, as she got back into the front passenger seat.

"There is an accident that is blocking half the road. Car versus bus. The police are directing traffic. We simply sit tight and wait out turn. Trust me, when I say, nobody is going to be arrested."

The line moved forward, the road tanker being the last vehicle through before a policeman held up a hand and stopped the traffic. It was another six minutes before their turn.

Once on *Autopista Nacional,* the Bel Air picked up speed.

"Is this a fast as you can go?" the American complained. "At this rate, we will never catch the tanker."

"Yes, it is," the Brazilian replied. "Although the bodywork of the vehicle is pristine, I don't think Father Marcolata spent money keeping the engine tuned. Relax, Harper, we'll spot the road tanker any minute now."

Forty minutes later, they were still hoping.

"It must have turned off," Karmina concluded.

"Just our bad luck, I guess," Harper replied philosophically. "Never mind. Let's go back to the apartment. There's always another day."

61

KIRT MITCHELL HAD BEEN TOLD THE MAZE OF TUNNELS, THAT housed Daniels' research complex, was not a place to go exploring on one's own. Nevertheless, being restricted to his billet, the mess hall, and recreation center were driving him crazy. He needed to take a walk.

Curious as to their original purpose, he recklessly proceeded down a side tunnel, which branched and branched again. Overhead, lamps appeared sporadic, but in truth, many of the bulbs had blown. Mitchell should have realized where he was heading was hardly ever visited by the rest of the personnel.

Water dripped on his head as he proceeded warily down another side tunnel. *Is this the fourth or fifth turn I've made?* Mitchell asked himself. Regardless, he walked on, expecting to find an answer at any moment.

He took another branch that came to a sudden end, blocked by a curved sheet of steel that looked like the exposed part of an enormous vertical cylinder. At the base was a heavy-duty access hatch, rectangular in shape, with a lever that secured two sizable latches. Similar doors reminded Mitchell of sealed watertight compartments on a warship.

He pushed up on the lever and then pulled. The metal groaned as the hatch reluctantly opened. Surprisingly, inside a half-dozen light bulbs still burned, taking the route of a ladder that permitted an upward climb to the ceiling. At the top, a large slab of concrete blocked off the end of the cylinder at the surface.

So why the ladder? Mitchell wondered. Again, he looked up. A blob of water hit him in the eye. "Damn it." He moved to the side, still looking upward. Cast in shadow was a smaller round hatch, just large enough to permit a man to squeeze through.

Maybe this is a possible way out? After a closer inspection, the ladder showed its lower rungs badly rusted, Mitchell dismissed the idea, deciding not to risk his life to a sudden fall. He turned and made his way back through the main hatch.

Attempting to retrace his route, he passed a small alcove he had not noticed before. By the dim light, he saw a stack of steel boxes. Some had fallen and spilled their contents; field telephones. Next to them were half-a-dozen reels of military-grade telephone wire. He picked up three of them. Quickly, Mitchell doubled back and tied the end of the first reel to the silo's door. Backtracking, he began panning out the wire as he went.

For nearly three hours, Mitchell felt he was trapped in a rabbit warren, wondering if he would ever find an exit. During that time, he had explored much of the network of passages. Not by choice, mind you, making numerous fruitless excursions that deadened. The panned-out cable helped him retrace his steps. False exits he marked off, using his boot to scratch a large X on the floor so that he would not venture down those passages again.

Finally, he heard the comforting shouts of people. Mitchell headed toward the sound.

Passing a small branch tunnel, Mitchell stopped. Nearest to him were a couple of discarded chairs, with their legs bent or broken off. Behind lay a stack of dinner plates, the china scratched or chipped through repeated use. Almost buried by the confusion of garbage, he saw an old commercial oven. Further back lay a veritable graveyard of computer hardware dating from the 1990s to the present day.

Almost at the central tunnel once more, he came across a deep recess set into the wall. Inside, a gigantic boring machine was parked. Mitchell examined it carefully, finding a small aluminum plate pop-riveted onto one side. Rubbing it clean with his fingers, he saw what he took to be the manufactures name: **Мосметрострой**. The next two lines gave a serial number and year of manufacture: **1958**. These tunnels were contracted by or with the supervision of Russian engineers, some time during or after 1958.

Mitchell was distracted by the whine of an electric vehicle. Following the curve, much to his relief, he had reached the main underground thoroughfare.

Another cart passed, loaded with a dozen or more corpses, still dripping with water. Dressed in white onesies, they were similar to those he had seen floating in the vat. *What was the term Daniels had used? Test subjects? Yes, that was the phase. A cold, indifferent description for people who had just died.*

An involuntary shiver went through Mitchell's body as he imagined their burial in an unmarked mass grave, never to be found by friends or families.

62

"WHATEVER ARE YOU LOOKING AT?" HARPER ASKED FEDERICO, WHO was sitting on the couch in Karmina's apartment. Not watching television or working on Batista's biography, the Brazilian's usual pastimes, he was using Seong-ho's laptop computer.

"Reviewing the recording made by the drone at the derelict power plant, if you must know. I'm checking whether or not there is an exposed part of the nuclear reactor that could cause my hair to fall out."

"And your balls to shrink to the size of cherry pips."

The Korean cracked up, having overheard the conversation while he was making himself a cup of coffee. "Honestly, Federico, the reactor was never installed. Surely you knew that? With the fall of the Soviet Union, the money from Moscow dried up. The whole project died a death in September of '92. Even the main turbine was removed in 2004 to replace one damaged at the *Guiteras* thermoelectric plant. As we saw, the whole place is a shambles."

"Except for the water treatment plant." Harper reminded them.

"And who did a good job of wrecking that?" the Brazilian's asked, as he continued watching the computer screen.

"Don't blame me. How was I to know the roof of the enclosure would not take my weight?"

"Stop making excuses, Harper. Come over here and take a look at this." Federico had paused the video at the point when the drone was tumbling towards the ground. "What's that building over there?"

Harper picked up the monitor and turned it sixty degrees until the ground was horizontal. "Beats me. Might be a boiler house, with a tall chimney, although it doesn't appear to be part of the original construction work."

Intrigued, the Korean came over to look for himself.

"What do you think, Seong-ho?"

Moon put down his coffee mug. "Reminds me of a crematorium, if you want my opinion. Why someone would build one there, I haven't a clue."

"A crematorium. You know, I believe you're right," said Federico. "Hold on, and I'll show you why."

Federico, after retrieving Karmina's computer from her desk, took less than a minute to *Google* a photograph of *Krema IV* at *Auschwitz-Birkenau*, taken in 1943.

"There's no similarity," Harper objected. "The chimney at *Auschwitz* was constructed with bricks. At *Juraguá*, from prefabricated steel piping."

"I'm not looking at that," Federico replied. "Focus on the roofs and the walls of nearby buildings. They are all coated in soot or black tar. It's the same in the picture and on the video."

"If you're right, Federico, it means Daniels is disposing of the bodies there. We should go check it out," Harper suggested. "Maybe we will find a clue as to his home base."

"And while we're there, we can search for the drone and pick up the crossbows," Seong-ho proposed.

"That is just great. I cannot wait for another chance to be exposed to more radiation," the Brazilian complained. "Do you think I should take a couple of aspirin before we leave?"

63

FEDERICO HAD TO FILE HIS WEEKLY COLUMN WITH THE ASSOCIATED Press Agency, which delayed the return visit to the abandoned *Juragua* power plant by a day.

While Karmina went to retrieve the crossbows, the others began their search for the drone. With Harper taking point, they began a stealthy reconnaissance, moving in an anti-clockwise direction, skirting the blockhouse. A third of the way around, they saw the golden sand that was the beach. Two enormous concrete pipes jutted out from the tropical vegetation, their inflows nose-deep amongst the crashing waves. Ignoring them, Harper pushed into the underbrush, ducking beneath trailing fronds, following a crude path that had become obscured with years of disuse. Federico and Seong-ho followed, close on his heels.

A thick cloud of mosquitoes arose from a black, algae-covered pond of stagnant water as he passed. The insects outnumbered them a thousand to one. Any effort to remain inconspicuous abandoned, the trio sprinted through the swarm, waving their arms, slapping hard at exposed skin, not stopping until they reached a grassy clearing.

Ahead, the supposed crematorium was less than thirty yards

away. Slowly they approached, weaving their way through a dumping ground of rusted machinery, most likely never used. Thankfully, no guards were waiting to challenge them.

As chance would have it, the downed drone was a few feet away from the building itself. After making a cursory inspection, Seong-ho informed his companions, "There's a crack in the casing. Nothing duck tape can't fix, however," he assured them.

"What about the missing propeller?" Federico asked.

"No problem. With the 3-D printer I've brought with me, I can easily replicate a new one."

A soon as Karmina caught up, all four of them entered the structure through a carelessly secured door with its padlock left unfastened. Instantly, a putrid smell, like rotting fish mixed with burning tires, assaulted their nostrils.

An open oven door revealed the remains of ash and small bone. Next to it was a machine for grinding up the large bones that were not consumed by the heat of the furnace. In one corner were several sacks filled with what looked like blackened bonemeal. The Korean removed his smartphone and took pictures.

"Definitely a crematorium," Harper concluded. "All we have to do now is find out where the bodies came from."

"So, where do we look?" Federico asked.

"We start by finding out the places were people have recently gone missing," Harper replied, "and plot them on a map. Federico, as a journalist, do you have a contact in the police department, who would supply you with that sort of information?"

64

GRATEFUL TO BE BACK AT THE MAIN COMPLEX, MITCHELL MADE his way towards his billet. To his surprise, Günter was sitting on his bunk, waiting.

Without asking where he had been, the Argentinian told him, "Kirt, over the next day or two, it's all hands on deck."

"Why? What's going on?"

"The *Doktor* needs to replenish his stock of subjects."

That word again, thought Mitchell.

Günter continued, "Daniels has perfected the injectable serum, and his tests have been going well. However, to teleported larger objects, the *Doktor* has increased the voltage. The problem is it's killing the patients."

We're calling them patients now, are we? Mitchell winced internally at the callousness behind the remark, wishing he had never got involved with Hyde or Daniels in the first place. Then an idea crossed his mind. *Perhaps there is a way to ease these poor creatures' suffering.* "Hmmm."

Fostering a deep loathing for this poker-playing wastrel, the Argentinian inquired impatiently, "What exactly do you mean by *hmm?*"

"I have a suggestion I need to share with Daniels. Where is he at the moment?"

"I warn you, Mitchell, don't go wasting the *Doktor's* valuable time. Right now, his temper is on a very short fuse."

"Let me worry about that," Mitchel countered. "Tell me."

"I believe he's supervising the change out of test subjects. We're using the last of the current batch."

"Thanks." Without further comment, Mitchell smiled, turned, and left.

Günter shouted after him, "Where do you think you're going? Come back. I haven't finished talking."

Daniels, however, was no longer in the chamber where he conducted his experiments. Mitchell found him in his office.

"Doctor, I'm sorry to disturb you, but …"

"Can't you see I'm busy? If it's about your assignment, Günter will fill you in on the details."

"He has already, thank you, sir." Sitting down without being invited, Mitchell continued, "I've come about the *patients*."

"What about them, man?" Daniels asked, irritated by the interruption. "They are dead; brain hemorrhages. I thought I'd got it right. However, once you bring me more subjects, with some slight tweaks, I'm positive I shall succeed." As if he had only just noticed, Daniels asked, "And who told you to sit down?"

"I've come about these tweaks you've just mentioned, sir. I have an idea."

"Mitchell, you are trying my patience. You are not a scientist. Remind me again what you were doing when we first met. Ah, I remember. You were a card sharp, or was it a shark? Whichever. Now, leave. You are interrupting my work."

"I believe one way of increasing the illumination in a room is by installing light bulbs with a higher wattage. A feeble comparison, I know, but isn't that what you've been doing with your subjects, attempting to increase their brainpower?" Mitchell spoke in a quiet, measured voice.

"Well, that's one way of putting it. To increase the output, I pass a sequence controlled higher voltage through areas of their cerebral cortex to encourage the firing of the patient's synapses."

"Resulting in you frying their brains. Do I have that right?"

"What are you getting at? I've warned you before, Mitchell. If you are going to be insubordinate, then you'll join the …"

"The next batch." Mitchell smiled as he finished the Doctor's sentence. "On the other hand, if I come up with an alternative solution?" He then rubbed his thumb again his fingers, a gesture that he expected to receive payment for the suggestion.

"Go on."

"If one cannot increase the wattage of a light bulb, the alternative is to turn on more lamps. In your particular case, Doctor, have you considered adding, say, four more spokes to the cartwheel in that vat of yours?" Once again, Mitchell rubbed his fingers together and smiled.

65

"I DON'T CARE HOW MANY MEN YOU HAVE TO USE. I NEED THOSE test subjects now, Hans. Not tomorrow, not in a week, but right now," Daniels ranted. "Do you understand?"

"*Ja, Herr Doktor*. I'll get three teams on it straight away. I'll lead one, my brother the second, and Mitchell the third. Do you wish us to patrol the countryside as before?"

"Yes. Include the towns as well. Even the outskirts of Havana, if necessary. Men and women, it doesn't matter, as long as they are healthy and below the age of thirty. It's already dark outside, so get going."

"*Sofort* [Immediately], *Doktor*." The Argentine clicked his heels and was about to turn to face the door.

"And, Hans, ensure you closely supervise these local *campesinos* [peasant-farmers] you hired. I don't want any damaged goods."

FRUSTRATED BY THE NON-ARRIVAL OF THE INFORMATION THE Brazilian had promised to get from his police contact, Harper asked, "What's the delay? We've been waiting for two days now."

"This is Cuba and not the NYPD. Wheels turn more slowly in this country," Federico replied in a mellow voice, trying to calm the American down.

"Yeah, slowly is right, and on my dime too. How much did you pay this contact of yours, Federico?"

"The equivalent of five hundred American dollars."

"That's outrageous," Harper protested.

"That was the last of the money I brought with me," Seong-ho informed him.

"What! You've blown through the $50,000 already?" Harper was not a happy man.

"False documents, passport, driver's license, the equipment I purchased on the black market, the fishing boat; all come at a high price, Harper."

"You can say that again. Mexico and Cuba are supposed to be countries with a low cost of living. I guess I was wrong. I think I'll move to Singapore, where things are cheaper." Harper, having walked to the refrigerator to get a cold beer, slammed the door closed in frustration. "Have you guys any suggestions about what we might do in the meantime?"

"Go to a nightclub," was Federico's offering.

"Play cards," Karmina proposed.

"Bad idea. Harper cheats big time," Seong-ho reminded everyone. "Do they have movie theaters in Havana?"

"Sure, they do," the Brazilian confirmed with a smile.

"In Spanish," was Harper's veto.

"We could brainstorm ideas as to how we might find Daniels," Seong-ho proposed.

"Like what?" Harper was still in a bad mood.

"I know." The Korean pulled the paper he had found near the overturned road tanker from his wallet. He read the entries. "The truck driver keeps using the word *Almacén* in his time log. That has to be Daniels' base of operations."

"You could be right," Harper agreed, enthusiastically. "I, for one, have had enough of chasing my tail. Karmina, see if you can find the place on a map."

The Cuban, seemingly, ignored the request.

"What's the matter now? Is that too much to expect?"

Grinning, Karmina asked her boyfriend, "Shall I tell him, or will you?"

"You can," Federico responded. "I don't want to upset Harper and risk breaking up a *beautiful* friendship." The Brazilian could barely contain himself from bursting out in laughter.

"Oh, very well," Karmina relented. "*Almacén* is not the name of a town or city, Harper. In Spanish, it means depot or garage."

"That's that then," the American concluded. "Nice try, though, Seong-ho. I need a volunteer to go and buy some more beer."

"We've almost run out of money," Federico reminded Harper.

"About that, Federico. How do I wire funds to your Cuban bank account from Switzerland?"

THE INFORMATION ON THE MISSING PERSONS FINALLY ARRIVED.

Pinned onto a corkboard, attached to the wall in Karmina's apartment, were two maps. One showed the entire island, while the second, on a larger scale, showed Havana. In Federico's hand were copies of the official reports on abductions that had occurred over the past six weeks. Harper and Karmina were marking each location, using color-coded pushpins, as the Brazilian read the details out loud. Red denoted kidnappings during the last seven days, blue a week before that, yellow three and four weeks out, and lastly black for weeks five and six. Seong-ho stood on the opposite side of the room, taking in the overview as the work progressed, making brief summaries on a notepad.

Finally, with the plot complete, Harper turned to the Korean and asked, "Seong-ho, what profound conclusions have you made?"

"None, I'm afraid," was the candid reply.

"Seong-ho, I thought you were a math genius," Harper chided.

"I am," the Korean answered, immodestly. "Hold on a second." Moon walked over to the maps. "What I *do* notice, contrary to what one might expect, is the majority of abductions take place in low populated areas. Except for the past week, that is. Whoever is on the prowl has become blatantly reckless. For example, three young people are snatched outside a nightclub, in the tourist district of Havana, and bundled into an unmarked black van."

"Did anyone identify the kidnappers?" Harper asked.

After consulting the relevant record, Federico replied, "They all wore ski masks, so apart from being male; no."

"What about the van's number plate?" was Harper's next question.

"No luck there, I afraid," the Brazilian answered. "It was unreadable. Covered in mud, as were the wheels and sides of the van."

"Maybe that's significant," Seong-ho suggested, "indicating the vehicle frequently travels a dirt road."

"Half the island is dirt roads," Karmina counted. "That's of no use. We need something more definitive to go on."

"I know," the Korean proclaimed. "I've just remembered. Hold on a sec while I get my phone." He went over to the table, picked up the device, and pulled up the photos he had recently taken. Showing the trio, he declared, "What do you think?"

"We're back outside the nuclear plant and the makeshift crematorium. I don't see how that helps." Harper responded.

"Oh, sorry." Seong-ho swiped the images to the left until he found the one he specifically wanted. "Here, look. Read the wording on the sacks used to collect the ashes."

SAN CRISTÓBAL DE MAÍZ Y HARINA DEL MOLINO

[San Cristobal Corn and Flour Mill]

FIFTY-TWO MILES DIRECTLY SOUTHWEST OF *HAVANA, SAN CRISTÓBAL* is a city in the *Artemisa* Province of Cuba, with a population of over 72,000. Harper was not interested in demographics, or the gas station, or the convenience store they had passed five minutes after leaving motorway *Autopista Este-Oeste*. However, twenty yards further on, they found the mill. Inside, a man was tying off sacks of flour and loading them onto a dolly. Federico asked if he was the owner. Without a word, the *jornalero* [hired hand] pointed up the steep flight of wooden stairs to the upper floor.

The Brazilian had to shout over the noise of the machinery to attract the attention of the man shoveling maize into a hopper.

"We're looking for someone who buys a lot of flour from you. Maybe on a weekly or monthly basis," was the translation. "Can you help me?" Federico asked.

The owner shook his head, averting his eyes to the ground. Harper pulled a twenty-dollar bill from his trouser pocket, flattened it out and waved it in front of the man.

"*No quiero ningún problema, señor. No puedo ayudarte* [I don't want any trouble, sir. I cannot help you]."

"Come on. We are not going to learn anything here," Harper decided. "Let's go find a place to eat. I'm starving."

"You could have offered him more money," Seong-ho suggested as they left the mill. "Money always talks, isn't that what they say?"

"Not in this case. The man is scared witless. He knows, but he isn't going to tell us," Harper responded.

"What are we going to do then? Sit around a wait for someone to arrive and load up with sacks of flour."

"The *cafeteria* across the street seems the perfect place to do just that," Harper concluded as he, Federico, and Karmina began crossing the road, which left the Korean standing, looking back into the mill and wondering if the laborer might divulge something.

"Seong-ho, are you joining us?" Karmina called. "Or are you on a diet?"

There was hardly any attempt at conversation during the meal. Not making any progress, everyone felt dejected. Federico suggested they question other locals, the shopkeepers, for example. Harper thought it would be a waste of time if Daniels' henchmen had instilled a stranglehold of fear on the community.

The four of them ordered more beer. While Federico and Seong-ho were eyeing the legs of the waitress as she went to fetch their drinks, Harper gazed out of the window.

When the waitress returned, somewhat unexpectedly, Harper proposed a toast, "To the infamous Doctor Daniels. May your days be numbered. I think I know where you are hiding."

"How?" the Korean exclaimed. "No one else here has a clue."

"Maybe not you three. Me, however, *that's* an entirely different story." Harper smiled. "While you and Federico were admiring that pretty girl's calves, I saw a road tanker shoot by, one similar to the type that crashed near *Juragua*. Taking ionize water to Daniels' hideaway to be used in his experiments is my bet. I'll put money on his base being near here."

"We've seen nothing except farms and light industry," Federico reminded them.

"Karmina, you know the island better than any of us. Are they any caves or underground structures in the vicinity?"

"I'm not sure, Harper. Let me think." There was a brief pause. "*É isso aí!* [That's it!] I do recall, during the time of the Cuban missile crisis, a couple of launch sites somewhere nearby. I remember reading that an American U-2 spy plane had photographed transporters for surface-based missiles, fueling vehicles, and erector equipment. However, I believe the Soviets were planning to build underground silos. For all I know, they may have started constriction before they withdrew completely."

"Seong-ho, did you bring your computer with you?"

"Yes, Harper. And the satellite link as well. They're in my backpack, which I left in the car."

"Great. Why don't you go and fetch them? Then we can use the Internet to check things out."

As soon as the Korean had his computer connected to the *World Wide Web*, he started by selecting Google Maps. Looking over Seong-ho's shoulder, the group spent fifteen minutes carefully reviewing satellite images of the area. There were numerous buildings within the city limits and the sounding townships, used for residential or small-scale manufacturing purposes. Seeking something more isolated, they searched the countryside and saw scattered dwellings and farm buildings, but nothing of any size presented itself.

Disgruntled, Harper was about to give up when Karmina suggested they needed a different approach. "Seong-ho, search under *San Cristóbal* and see if anything of interest comes up."

The results gave information about cigar brands, the Municipality, restaurant reservations, the weather forecast, and much more, but nothing relevant caught their eye.

"Type *'San Cristóbal Cuban missile crisis'*", Federico proposed.

Seong-ho complied.

And there it was, out of 16,000 results, an article halfway down page 1 :

October 23, 1962: Photo of San Cristobal Medium Range Ballistic Missile (MRBM) site in Cuba...

Somewhere near *San Cristóbal* was an underground complex housing missile silos. The big question, however, was the exact location.

After more searching, finally, they hit pay dirt. As well as showing bunkers, buildings, silos, and the tunnel entrance, all labeled, one photograph gave a grid reference as well.

22°41'07.4"N 83°14'03.9"W

The Korean punched in the coordinates into the browser's search bar, and bingo, what they were looking for was less than eleven miles west as the crow flies, fourteen miles by road.

They parked a mile short of the identified site and began walking parallel but away from the track. The going was slow, for the formerly cultivated plots of land, now abandoned, had been reclaimed by Mother Nature. Upon finding a grove of wild banyan trees, which provided excellent cover, Seong-ho began setting up the drone. Within a few minutes, it was airborne. Everyone watched apprehensively as the video monitor displayed what the camera saw.

Several vehicle tracks extended for a couple of hundred yards, before turning into a smallholding dominated by two large commercial greenhouses. Amongst them, the distinctive tanker's trends stood out in the dust, turning north for twenty yards or so, then making a sharp right before disappearing, seemingly to nowhere.

"Go down low and come at it head-on," Harper instructed. "That's it, Seong-ho. That's his lair. Now we know the Doctor's secret bunker."

They were looking at the downward sloping entrance into a tunnel.

"Harper, you're not suggesting we go in there and confront the man?" Federico asked during the debate on how to proceed.

"I'm proposing we do just that," the American replied.

"But that's suicide. God knows how many men Daniels has with him. They're probably all armed to the teeth."

"Not to worry," Harper responded, jocularly. "What were need are reinforcements, so that we can fight fire with fire. And I think I know just where to find them."

THE FOLLOWING MORNING, KARMINA AND HARPER, HAVING DRIVEN along *Avenida 5ta,* and turned onto *Calle* 70, parked the Chevrolet in front for *Centro Comercial* supermarket, which was on the corner of *3ra.* From there, it was a short walk to the Russian embassy.

"Are you going inside?" Karmina asked.

"Hardly," the American replied. "If they knew I was part of the debacle that erupted after we left their submarine *Zaporizhzhia* moored in Havana harbor all those years ago, I'd be flown to Moscow in a diplomatic pouch."

"So, what's the plan, Harper?"

"We wait outside the gates, and stop the first friendly looking Russian and ask them if there is an enclave of Soviet expatriates in the city."

"And how will you know if they are Russian?" Karmina asked.

"Apart from looking sad, they will be chain-smoking," the American assured her.

"I don't know that," the Cuban responded.

"Neither did I, until Federico told me."

"But is it true, Harper?"

"We're about to find out. Here comes one now."

The person they spoke to told them there were approximately a thousand Russians, more if one counted their descendants, living on the island. Where they were living in Havana, she could not say specifically. However, in a thick Slavic accent, she did suggest they try one or two restaurants that serve Russian cuisine. Hence, the pair found themselves sitting at a table of *Nazdarovie*, on *Malecón*. Harper chose his seat so that he had a view of the whole room and could easily see people arriving and leaving.

With black chairs and tables, the place followed the retro Soviet-style furnishings of eighty years ago. A large poster, set behind the bar, depicted a pair of hands clasped together. Below were the letters **СССР · Куба**, and below them the Soviet and Cuban flags.

"What does CCCP stand for?" Harper asked the waiter as he brought their first course.

"Союз Советских Социалистических Республик," he was told. "CCCP is an abbreviation. Translated it means *Union of Soviet Socialist Republics*."

"So now you know," Karmina said lightheartedly. "This food is delicious. Have you spotted anyone you know?"

"Not yet," Harper replied, which he amended to a simple *no* when they readied to leave. "This is worse than searching for a needle in a haystack."

"Then I suggest we look elsewhere," Karmina told him, still in a cheerful mood. "There's another poster behind you, to your left. It's a picture of a cathedral."

Catedral Ortodoxa Nuestra Señora de Kazán, in Russian, Православный Собор Богоматери Казанской, was consecrated on October 19th, 2008. While Harper was admiring the Byzantium architecture, in Spanish, Karmina asked the deacon where the Russian community resided in Havana. "All over," she was told, "but if you attend Sunday mass, you will be able to see many of them. Invariably, the attendance is good."

As well as Harper and Julia, Seong-ho was one of the prisoners rescued from the converted oil rig by the submarine. He, therefore, knew its crew and was in Havana when they split-up. The majority returned to Russia, a few went to Italy and Sicily, and the remainder chose to live in Cuba. It, therefore, made sense, when, three days later, it was the Korean standing next to Harper as the congregation swarmed out the cathedral, like bees exiting a hive.

"We'd best separate," Harper suggested. "They're going in all directions. Meet me back here in fifteen minutes."

Harper stood impatiently, wishing there was a wall clock in view. He estimated he had been waiting for more than half an hour. "Where are you, Seong-ho?" he muttered. "You should have returned by now."

The American slowly made a full three-sixty-degree turn, scanning the faces of passers-by. As he looked towards the street, he saw a black Mercedes parked on the far side. He remembered Karmina's neighbor had trailed a black Mercedes into the mountains and wondered if it was the same vehicle. He stared, trying to see the faces behind the darkened windows. Then the car drove off.

As the Korean approached, Harper voiced his concern. "I was beginning to worry." Then he recognized the two men at Seong-ho's side. "Well, I never. Nikolai, Petya, it's good to see you. How are you?"

"*Zdravstvuj* [Hello], Harper. *Nichyego* [So-so], but what can you expect at our age." The exchange of words was accompanied by the Slavic greeting of a bear hug and kisses on the cheeks from Petya.

Too much, Harper decided.

Nikolai, did the same but followed up with a hearty slap on the back.

Mentally Harper reaffirmed, *Way, way too much.*

Reunions concluded, Seong-ho explained that he had spotted Petya leaving the church. Of the former submariners who stayed in Cuba, only one other had remained in Havana.

"So what took you so long to get back here?" the American asked.

"Petya took me to find Nikolai. His home is but a short distance from the cathedral."

"I have to rest foot on doctor orders. But to see old friend, I make exception," the Russian explained in broken English.

"Nikolai has gout. Drinks too much alcohol," Petya elaborated.

"I drink less beer," the other Russian protested. "I do as doctor says. I very good patient."

"And more sodas." Petya reminded him. "Sugar bad for you."

"Pshaw," Nikolai responded contemptuously. "At my age, who cares? Come, my friends. I drink your health. My wife says no vodka in house, but in bar I think is okay."

SEONG-HO, UNABLE TO STAND THE GRINDING OF GEARS, HAD ELECTED to take over the driving.

"What do you think of the two old codgers?" Harper asked as they headed towards Karmina's apartment

"They are good at spinning tall tales. Did their commander really trade a bottle of *Stolichnaya* vodka for the release of a British frigate from the *Severomorsk* naval base?"

"It happened sometime in the 1960s, apparently," Harper replied. "But not quite the way those two rascals described it. I believe a British submarine was sent to beat the drum. However, their version sounded much funnier."

"Do you think they can help us defeat Doctor Daniels and his guards?" the Korean asked.

"At their age? That is most unlikely. I'll wager, both Nikolai and Petya need assistance getting dressed in the morning."

"They did offer to bring some rifles."

Harper laughed. "And some torpedoes, if I remember correctly. Mind you, after four shots of vodka, they'd have offered us a ballistic missile if the could get their hands on one. However, in truth, I think their presence would be more a hindrance than a help."

"So what do we do now?" was the Seong-ho's next question.

"I'll think of something. Just drive."

"Slow down, Seong-ho. Take the next left."

"But that's not the way to the apartment."

"I know, but a black Mercedes has been on our tail for the past five minutes. What's more, it is not making any effort to hide. Take another left, down that narrow street."

Seong-ho complied and continued taking instructions until the Mercedes was no longer in sight.

"When I give the word, pull over. Get ready to leave the car quickly. We're going to abandon the Chevy and proceed on foot," Harper explained.

"Is that wise? On foot, they will easily catch up with us."

"Don't argue. Stop right here," Harper insisted.

Exiting the vehicle, Harper taking the lead, the pair sprinted towards the confusion of tourists that thronged the area.

"Across the street," the American yelled breathlessly. "Make for that alleyway. The Mercedes is too wide to follow."

"Okay, I think we're good. We've shaken off our pursuers." Harper stopped at a payphone positioned on a street corner and began to dial.

"Who are you calling?" Seong-ho inquired.

"First for a taxi. While we are waiting for it to arrive, I'll ring Federico and inform him the apartment is under surveillance. He and Karmina should leave under cover of darkness, and not take the Lada."

"Where should they go?"

Harper did not answer straight away. Looking over the rooftops of the dwellings opposite, he had sight of the tower and pinnacles of a building he recognized; *Iglesia del Santo Ángel Custodio.*

"Harper?" said Seong-ho.

No response.

Santo Ángel Custodio. Harper repeated the phrase in his mind. The nucleus of an idea was slowly forming, which would give him an alternative to recruiting the Russian submariners.

"Harper?" the Korean repeated, more loudly.

"What?"

"You didn't answer my question. Where should Federico and Karmina go, once they have left the apartment?"

"Oh, that. The same place we are, Seong-ho. To My Father's house."

THE SOUND OF A MOTORCYCLE'S ENGINE CAUSED HARPER AND Seong-ho to step out of the presbytery, formerly occupied by the late Father Marcolata. Federico was steering a battered Soviet-built *Karpaty*, with Karmina riding pillion.

The American was relieved, having given explicit instructions for Federico not to use the *Suzuki* Seong-ho had ferried to the island. Karmina's neighbor had agreed to swap motorcycles after the Brazilian explained it was a way of saying thank you for him tracking the Mercedes as far as *La Sierrata*.

"Better get the motorcycle out of sight, Federico," Harper suggested, "and then you should come inside."

The church itself remained in a state of disarray. Thankfully the priest's body had been removed from the presbytery. Someone had made a halfhearted attempt at cleaning the bloodstains from the wall and floor.

Harper and Seong-ho began straightening the furniture and returning the books to the shelves. Disconcertingly, there was no hotplate, kitchenware, crockery, or utensils. Table lamps were gone, as were the priest's clothes, bedding, even the light bulbs, all, presumably, stolen.

"Looks like we need to make a trip to the store if we're going to stay here," said Harper. "Do you have any money left, Seong-ho?"

"A few pesos," the Korean replied. "That's not going to buy very much."

"In that case, tomorrow, Federico needs to take the motorcycle and drive into the city. Those funds I wired into his bank account should be available for withdrawal by now."

"How much should I take out?" the Brazilian asked.

"That's simple," the American replied. "All of it."

HANS STOOD IN FRONT OF DANIELS' DESK, WAITING FOR THE TIRADE that he knew was about to happen. He could tell the Doctor had a full head of steam by the way his boss breathed heavily through his mouth rather than his nostrils.

"You and your brother, you're both utter nincompoops. How could you lose them? Huh? Tell me that."

"They abandoned their car and darted down a backstreet packed with pedestrians, *Herr Doktor*. We were unable to follow."

"You've lost the use of your legs now, I suppose. Total *Schafsköpfe* [blockheads], the pair of you. I suppose you were following too closely, and they spotted you?"

The Argentinian stood there, nervously wringing his hands together.

"I take it from your silence that's a yes. Did you check the apartment?"

"Ja, *Doktor*. Bernhart checked the next day. The Brazilian and the woman are gone."

Daniels rose to his feet. "Do we know where Harper and Moon went?"

"No, sir. We don't have the people for twenty-four-hour

surveillance. But the Lada and the Suzuki motorcycle are still parked outside in the square. Surely, they will be back."

The Doctor scoffed. " That is no guarantee, Hans. Those are not the only two vehicles in Havana. Anything else to report?"

Hans squeezed his hands tighter, wishing this conversation was over. "I checked around the water treatment plant after the roof caved in, and found a piece of a propeller. The kind used by a small drone."

"Sounds like Harper has been snooping around there too. Did the guards see anyone?"

"They seem reluctant to say anything at all."

"Which means they either were sleeping on the job or sitting in the shade," Daniels concluded. "No matter. Soon I shall be ready for the final test. If successful, I will have no more need for ionized water, not here in Cuba anyway. I never knew what my father saw in the place. I'll be glad to get off this wretched island."

"Do you think Harper knows about this facility, sir?"

"How could he?" Daniels snapped back in reply. "There's no reason to think he'll come snooping around *San Cristóbal*. If he does, the locals know the consequences if they don't keep their mouths shut." The Doctor pulled the edge of his hand across his throat as if it were a knife. "However, it would be prudent to increase security. Go into town and round up some local thugs. Put guns in their hands. We must present a show of force to that *Schweinhund* and his cronies if they show up here."

"Is that wise, *Herr Doktor*? Without proper training, if they start shooting the place up, people could be killed."

"As long as that includes Harper and his accomplices, I don't care. Now, make arrangements. I want more guards in place as soon as possible."

The Argentinian turned to leave.

"One more thing, Hans. Has my guest arrived yet?"

"*Nein, Herr Doktor*. His plane has been delayed. He is expected to land at *Playa Baracoa* Airport this afternoon."

"Very good. Let me know as soon as my financial backer gets here. He'll be delighted to see the progress I have made."

75

HARPER WAS AMAZED AT HOW QUICKLY THE NEW FUNDS BECAME depleted. Having itemized the expenditure, converted to US dollars, he went down the list:

- Payment to 30 dancers ... $ 30,000
- Timber and labor ... $ 2,500
- Steel panels and welding ... $ 2,800
- Miscellaneous ... $ 250
- Charitable donation ... $ 3,000
- Hiring a bus and driver ... $ 1,000
- Van Hire ... $ 400
- Banker's fee ... $ 5,000
- Household items ... $ 650

"Incredible. I cannot believe we've spent $45,600, Federico. What's this charitable donation of $3,000 all about?"

"The smoke grenades you wanted. From my police contact."

"And the banker's fee?"

The Brazilian laughed. "A little something to encourage the bank manager not to report the transaction to the authorities."

"Mmm," Harper replied. "Remind me to come back as a banker in my next life. So how's the construction going?"

"It will be a few days before the steel sheeting arrives. Apart from that, the framework and paper mache are finished. Just need a paint job."

"And the dancers? Are we on for next weekend?"

"Not Saturday. Too many want to watch baseball. Sunday, after church, is okay. We'll need to provide them with lunch. It's budgeted for under miscellaneous."

"It appears we are almost ready then. Are you planning to attend the church service before we leave?"

The Brazilian looked at Harper in surprise. "I hadn't planned to. Are you?"

"Yes. I don't think it will do any harm to have God on our side. After all, we need all the help we can get."

76

"GREAT-AUNT CORDELIA COME QUICK. MOM'S ON THE FRONT lawn, acting weird." Oliver shouted as he ran along the hallway and into the kitchen.

Cordelia put down the dough she was kneading, wiped her hands on her apron, and, using her walking cane, followed the boy as quickly as she was able to the front door. They joined Spencer, who was standing on the stoop.

"What's going on?" Cordelia asked, upon seeing her niece swirling around and around as if she were Maria in *The Sound of Music*.

"Aunt Julia started doing that as soon as she'd finished her phone call," Spencer said. "Is she ever going to stop?"

"Julia," Cordelia cried. "Julia!"

Oliver's mother ceased her gyrations and walked over, be it not in a straight line, for in truth, she had made herself quite dizzy. Reaching the outdoor couch, she said breathlessly, "I think I had better sit down," and flopped onto the cushions.

"Before you fall over, you mean. Whatever have you been doing?"

"Listening to the best news I've heard in ages," Julia replied. "I was speaking with Mike Jones of the FBI."

"So what does the FBI have to say for themselves?"

"They've traced the money taken from our Swiss bank account."

Cordelia scoffed. "You must have connections in high places, to have them monitor your finances. How much went missing?"

"One hundred thousand dollars."

Oliver whistled through the gap in his front teeth.

"Olly, stop that, please. I am trying to have a serious conversation with your great-aunt."

"Okay," Oliver acknowledged.

"That is a lot of money. Did they catch the thief?" Cordelia asked.

"Not exactly, Aunty. Someone I know, who lives in California, received half the funds. Not so sure about the rest, though." For a second, there was a touch of self-doubt in Julia's voice.

"Do you know where the balance ended up?" Cordelia asked, as the children, having become bored with listening to the adult conversation, ran onto the lawn and began imitating Julia's twirls.

"A bank in Cuba."

"Cuba!" Cordelia exclaimed in surprise. "That's where Roger tried to rescue prisoners during a cellblock fire." The aunt sucked in a breath, realizing she resisted a subject better left unvoiced. Cordelia sat down on the couch and placed a hand on Julia's arm. "I'm so sorry. I shouldn't have … You know what I mean."

"Don't be. Roger is the one who gave instructions to move the money. Which means it's further proof he's still alive." Julia's face was beaming with joy.

"I don't think I've seen you look so radiant all the time you've been staying here. Are you sure it was Roger?"

"Ninety-nine percent positive. Agent Jones has agreed to fly to Cuba and personally check things out." Julia put her arms around her aunt, and they hugged one another. Then Julia started to cry tears of happiness, which was only drowned out by the sound of Oliver and Spencer's laughter and the dog's barking.

PARKED IN FRONT OF THE CHURCH OF *SANTO ÁNGEL CUSTODIO*, thirty Cubans boarded the commandeered school bus, with the faded words *TRANSPORTE ESCOLAR* painted on the sides. Despite the ban on alcohol, they were in a festive mood. Harper had recruited some of the participants from the parade of the Guardian Angel, explaining one of his friends was having a party in some caverns southwest of the city. He wanted to give him a birthday surprise by frightening him with a giant effigy of *El Coco*, the bogeyman.

After the men were seated, using Federico as the translator, Harper went over his plan. He emphasized his friend was somewhat eccentric, and, coming from Texas, would sometimes shoot first and ask questions later. "If bullets start to fly," he told them, "everyone is to take shelter at the foot of the statue."

"¡Si un gringo loco quiere jugar juegos estúpidos con otro gringo loco, *me resbala!* [If one crazy gringo wants to play stupid games with another crazy gringo, I don't care!]," one of the participants declared. Why should he, or anyone else on the bus for that matter? They each had twenty-five thousand pesos in their pockets, equivalent to one thousand American dollars. With the average wage in Cuba being seven hundred and fifty pesos a month, they had received a small fortune.

Having checked that everyone had brought their costume and mask, Harper handed out swimming goggles, with an assortment of red, greed, and blue lenses. "To make your eyes look scary," he explained, concealing the fact that Federico had procured half a dozen smoke grenades to throw if things got out of control. He also handed everyone a bandana, which he instructed be soaked in water and used to cover their mouths.

"*Un gringo loco* [One crazy American]," everyone told themselves.

It took two and a half hours to reach their objective, an overgrown track away from the greenhouses. Harper told the driver to park the bus under a tree. With a profusion of Spanish moss, it provided the perfect natural camouflage to conceal the vehicle.

Seong-ho pulled up behind the school bus and dismounted the *Karpaty*. He had refused to sit in the school bus or ride with Federico in the box van, claiming both were potential death traps. As if the Russian-built motorcycle was any safer.

The Brazilian parked the van at the rear of the mini convoy. By the time the Cubans had disembarked and assembled, he had the van's doors open and was ready for the statue to be unloaded.

Everyone donned their costumes and masks. With torches lit, the effigy was hoisted on to the shoulders of a dozen men. Harper took the lead. Twenty minutes later, the procession reached the tunnel entrance.

In the dim light of the overhead lamps, long shadows were cast both fore and aft. Green, red, and blue eyes glared out from behind the skull masks. *If Daniels' cronies aren't frightened*, Harper thought to himself, *this procession of ghouls certainly scares the crap out of me.*

"Duérmete niño, *[Sleep, my baby,]*
Duérmete ya *[Sleep, baby, do.]*
Que viene el coco *[The bogeyman's coming]*
Y te llevará.   *[And he will take you.]*

"Duérmete niño, *[Sleep, my baby,]*
Duérmete ya. *[Sleep, baby, do.]*
Que viene el coco *[The bogeyman's coming]*
Y te comerá. *[And he will eat you.]*"

AS THE CUBANS CHANTED, THE ACOUSTICS OF THE TUNNEL MADE AS though the men were singing a Gregorian chant. The statue gently swayed from side to side with each forward step. The torches flickered in the breeze that was the forced ventilation.

So far, so good, Harper thought as he crouched on the hoisted dais, hidden from view by the stature itself. No guards presented themselves. Not yet, anyway. The deeper their advance into the tunnel, before any confrontation, the better.

"Duérmete niño *[Sleep, my baby]*
Duérmete ya. *[Sleep, baby, do].*"

"Everything is going well," the Brazilian remarked as he walked alongside.

Federico spoke too soon. As they rounded the bend, fifty yards ahead, a line of guards blocked their path, each with a raised rifle.

Notwithstanding, the procession did not falter.

"Que viene el coco *[The bogeyman's coming]*
Y te llevará. *[And he will take you.]*"

Let's hope no one opens fire, Harper prayed, as each stride brought them nearer to Daniels' lair. *Sleep, my baby. Stay nice and quiet. Nobody needs to get shot. That's it. Sleep, my baby, do.*

"Que viene el coco, *[The bogeyman's coming,]*
Y te comerá. *[And he will eat you.]*"

WHEN KIRT MITCHELL SAW THE DEFENSE OF THE UNDERGROUND
complex was going badly, he was one the first to break ranks.
Together with many of locally recruited guards, he dashed past the
column of masked assailants. Unlike the *guajiros*, he was not
superstitiously shouting, "*Correr. Correr. El Coco te atrapará* [Run. Run.
The bogeyman will get you]." Unlike them, he did not rush blindly
into a side tunnel. He chose his escape route with care, selecting the
one where lay the spooled out telephone wire used to assist his
return to the main tunnel.

Heading for the silo, Mitchell paused long enough at the
scrapheap to snap off a chair leg, before running as fast as he could,
putting as much distance between himself and the melee that was
behind him.

He forked left and left again, followed by a right and another
right. Mitchell's pace slowed as he became out of breath. The
confusion of men shouting fell away, leaving the sound of dripping
water and his own footsteps. However, that was not all.

Someone was running towards him, in a skipping motion as he
favored one leg, no doubt using the same cabling as a guide rope.

One more turn and Mitchell saw the convex barrier that was the side of the cylinder. As he pulled open the hatch, a man appeared at the end of the tunnel. Without hesitation, Mitchell stepped inside, closed the latch, and jammed the chair leg between the metal paneling and the leveler.

Mitchell started to climb.

He was a third of the way up when he head humping fists against the locked steel door. Mitchell grinned, looked up towards his salvation, and once more resumed his ascent.

"Damn it," Seong-ho cursed as he kicked the plating several times. He tried pulling up on the lever. It would not budge. The Korean took a dozen paces back and then ran towards the door, hitting it with his left shoulder. There was the sound of clanking steel as the chair-leg dislodged and fell to the concrete floor. Seong-ho pulled on the lever again. The hatch swung towards him. He was inside.

The clatter of the chair leg had caused Mitchell to stop. He looked down. The face of the man who had visited Julia Harper was looking up. Deciding this was not the time to exchange greetings, once more he resumed the climb. Boots against metal rungs intensified as two men ascended the ladder.

Seong-ho, seemingly having the agility of a mountain goat, was moving at twice the pace of Mitchell. Notwithstanding, time was running out to close the gap.

Now at the top of the ladder, Mitchell opened the exit hatch to the surface and climbed through. Seong-ho had done well and was less than twenty feet below him. Pausing long enough to give his pursuer the finger, the card shark sprinted away into the brush.

"Son of a bitch!" Seong-ho exclaimed as he redoubled his efforts. "You're not getting away from me."

The protests of a bracket pulling away from the silo wall caused the Koran to slow his climb. Another. Then another. As he moved, the ladder began to sway, ever so slowly swinging out and away from the silo wall. The pinging sound of bolts hitting the ground was the last of his concerns. In a few more seconds, the whole of the ladder would come crashing down.

Scrambling up the last few rungs, the Korean was now directly below the center of the hatchway. It was now or never. With a leap, he grasped hold of the lip. The ladder fell away, and Seong-ho was left dangling, admiring the drop of ninety feet to the floor.

The Korean flexed his arm muscles and managed to pull himself up so that his chin was higher than the hatchway lip. Surrounded by low bushes and trailing vines, one fibrous stem was within his reach. In desperation, he grabbed at the stalk, praying it would not snap. Hand over hand, he pulled himself out.

Exhausted, Seong-ho lay on his back, looking up at the sky, grateful to be alive. The noise from a motorcycle starting up and then speeding away reached his ears. "Damm you again, Mitchell. You've stolen my ride."

THE MAJORITY OF GUARDS DESERTED WITHOUT A SINGLE SHOT FIRED. Those that remained, however, were not so passive. A hail of bullets, fortunately, all aimed at the statue and not the marchers, caused the paper mache skin to fragment into confetti. The polystyrene core fared no better. Harper felt as if he was standing before a blower, which was forcing insulation into a roof space, so dense were the snowflake-granulates.

"Okay. Stop right here," the American shouted. "Lower the statue to the ground. Everybody take cover behind the steel shield."

Karmina repeated the instructions in Spanish.

"What are we going to do now?" Federico asked as the gunfire continued.

"Get closer," Harper responded. "We'll push the statue forward like a sled. When we are near enough, we'll toss the smoke grenades. That should make the gunmen retreat."

"And if that doesn't work?" the Brazilian inquired, apprehensively.

"It will," Harper replied overconfidently. "Trust me."

Smoke, forced by the venation system, blew towards Harper and the interlopers. The defenders were unaffected.

Harper switched into mind-meld mode and communicated with the defenders to surrender. There was no ceasefire.

"Sweet Jesus; this isn't working." He yelled, "Federico, what's the Spanish for *I'm ordering you to surrender?*"

"Why do you want to know for, Harper?"

"This is not a debating society. Somebody tell me, please!"

Karmina came to his rescue, responding with, "*Te ordeno que te rindas.*"

Harper mentally transmitted the phrase. Bullets continued to ricochet off the now exposed bare-metal shielding. Chancing a glance around the barrier, the American saw the rearguard were wearing riot gear and helmets, no doubt lined with foil. *Damm it, Daniels. How come you think of everything?*

Over the noise, Harper shouted to Federico, "Get all the Cubans out of here before someone gets killed." Wasted words; they had already fled. With only the Brazilian and his girlfriend for company, things could hardly get any worse.

Or could they?

An object flew over the top of the steel plating, bounced once, and rolled slowly along the floor towards them.

"Ah, Mr. Harper; enjoy our little nap, did we? The knockout gas, a little invention of mine, is practically instantaneous, with no after-effects. Welcome to the party."

Harper, who found himself sitting in a chair, had his hand movement restricted by plastic restraints. He lifted his head and looked at his surroundings. He was inside the chamber that housed a large vat. Bodies floated face upward in the water, spaced out like the spokes of a wheel. Snaking cables, attached via electrodes, linked each subject to a central control console.

"Let me make the introductions."

Harper switched his gaze to the person speaking. "You unspeakable piece of shit, Daniels. What are you doing to the people in the tank?"

Ignoring the American's question, the doctor continued, "Hans, you know already, from our little fishing trip. Next to him is his brother, Bernhart. The gentleman standing at the control panel, his name is Günter. Been with me for twenty years. A loyal and trusty servant."

Harper responded with a look of disdain.

Daniels' only reaction was an all-knowing smile. "Come now, Mr. Harper, I'd expect a more cheery look than that from you. Your two friends are here. *Señor* Ramírez for one, although he's not here today as a member of the press corps. Instead, he's going to assist me in testing the next generation of analog computers. An unprecedented leap forward in design, I might add." Harper saw Federico standing on a suspended platform, in the center of the water tank, his eyes locked on the muzzle of the pistol Bernhart was holding. "And we mustn't forget your charming lady friend. Like you, she's here as an observer."

"She's not my lady friend," Harper hissed.

"Whatever you say," Daniels replied. "*Das ist mir Wurst* [It's all the same to me]. Günter, are we ready to proceed?"

"*Jawohl, Herr Doktor*. The countdown timer has been set. Upon your command, all I have to do is press the button."

"You're not going to get away with this. We've got back up."

"Mr. Harper, did your mommy never scold you for telling tall tales?" Daniels walked along the catwalk and stopped inches from where Federico was standing. "I don't hear any rescuers outside the doors; do you, Federico?"

The Brazilian did not reply.

"Not in a conversational mood today; is that it?"

Again no comment.

"I guess not. No matter. It's time to get things started." The Doctor turned away and instructed his orderly, "Günter, on my mark. One. Two. Three."

"Stop!" Harper exclaimed. "Put me in Federico's place."

The Doctor smiled. "Such a noble gesture. It reminds me of *A Tale of Two Cities*. I've always been a fan of Charles Dickens, you know. My English teacher, however, was so dismissive of the opening paragraph. All one sentence; one hundred and nineteen words, I recall her telling me. "*If that is an example of how to write, how can I expect my pupils to learn differently? Bad grammar,*" she'd said. What was the opening line?" Daniels put a finger to his lips as if he was seriously thinking. "Ah, yes, I remember. *It was the best of times, it was the worst of times, it was the age of wisdom, it was the age of foolishness.*

That so applies to me and you, Harper. Best for me, worse for you, my wisdom, your foolishness. Wouldn't you agree?"

Harper shook his head, amazed at the audacity of the man.

"You don't? Well, we're all entitled to our own opinions, I suppose. But I won't hold that against you. Request granted. Hans, help Mr. Harper out of his seat and make the swap."

Constrains removed, Harper stood up on his own, pushing away the Argentinian's hand that guided him onto the platform. Federico shuffled back to the small flight of stairs and stepped down onto the floor. He stood three feet away from the control panel.

"A little further to your left, Harper, if you please," the Doctor instructed. The American did not move. Daniels stepped onto the runway and walked nearer. "Don't make this harder than it needs to be."

Begrudging, Harper moved over.

"There. That wasn't so difficult, was it? Are you ready, Mr. Harper?" Daniels stepped closer and leaned in. "I wouldn't miss this moment for the world." The Doctor rubbed his hands together in anticipation, for what Harper knew not. The American's face must have betrayed his dismay, for Daniel added, "How rude of me. I haven't told you where you are going." Soliciting no response from Harper, he continued, "I've reserved a spot for you in the Bahamas. A nice sunny beach. I hope you arrive in one piece; or not." Daniels let out a manic laugh. "Time will tell."

"Go fuck yourself, Daniels," Harper replied.

"Language, Harper. Language. Remember, there is a lady present, those floating in the tank excepted. Okay, Günter. Are you ready?"

"All system nominal, *Doktor.*"

"Wait!" the American shouted. "I have a question before I leave."

"What is it now, Harper?"

"I was wondering what the word *Nootrop* means."

"This is hardly the time to give you a German lesson."

"Please, I'm curious. The word *Nootrop* was written on a scrap of paper I found in the Mazorra Asylum, Consider it my last request."

"Ironically, by finding that *scrap of paper, Herr* Harper, you unwittingly helped me tweaked my father's formula, which has been injected into the test-subjects below. So, by way of a thank you, I will tell you. *Nootrop* translates to *nootropic*. Nootropics are smart drugs, brain enhancers. But enough of your stalling, Harper. Günter, let's do this. Start the time now!"

A large digital clock on the wall flicked from 10 to 09.

"Time for you to leave, *Herr* Harper. *Auf Wiedersehen.*"

There was a resounding crash as Karmina sideswiped the chair formerly occupied by Harper, as she sprinted towards the platform.

07.

A handgun discharged.

"Stop shooting, you idiot," Daniels screamed at Bernhart. "You nearly hit me."

05.

Despite having his hands tied, Federico charged the control console, grabbing at knobs, twisting them, trying to stop the countdown.

02.

Günter struggled to reset the dials.

01, 00. *Poof.*

The sound of air suddenly filling a vacuum was the first indication that something had happened. A splash followed as Harper hit the water. Preoccupied wrestling each other, Günter and Federico missed the lightning-fast sequence of events.

Karmina had plowed into Daniels, instantly wrapping both arms around the Doctor's midsection. Inertia carried them onto the platform. They both struck Harper, sending him over the edge. As he fell, he glimpsed the pair locked together. Then the lights flickered off and back on. They were gone.

Once in the water, Harper began to panic as strands of cabling snared his legs. A hand brushed his face, and then another. Flailing wildly with his arms, he yelled, "Get your grubby paws off me."

"Relax, buddy. It's me," Federico reassured him.

The American felt himself being lifted out of the tank. After that, everything morphed into darkness.

8 2

"Roger, wake up." Harper thought the heard Julia's voice. "How are you feeling?"

Harper opened his eyes. A woman was smiling at him. "You're not Julia," were his first words. "You're ... Hold on; it will come to me. You're Special Agent Delaney. Where's your sidekick, Jones."

"Right here, Mr. Harper," a gruff voice responded. "You're a hard man to catch up with."

Harper looked at the two agents and then around the room. Federico was still there. Hans, Bernhart, and Günter as well, the three in handcuffs. Paramedics were lifting people from the tank and placing them on gurneys. Behind Jones stood an officious looking gentleman dressed in a police uniform.

"May I introduce *Primer Teniente* [Senior Lieutenant] Héctor Guillén, of the *Policía Nacional Revolucionaria* [National Revolutionary Police Force]? I am here merely in an advisory capacity," Special Agent In Charge Mike Jones added out of deference to the policeman.

"Why you, Jones, of all people?" Harper asked frostily. He had not forgotten how Jones and Delaney had escorted him to Cuba.

"Your wife asked me to check on your well-being."

"Wh … What? How is Julia involved?"

"Well, according to Mrs. Harper, you've been a naughty boy, recklessly withdrawing $100,000 for one of your joint accounts. To say she was upset is an understatement. Take my advice, and do like I do. Put your wife in charge of the household budget. It stops all that domestic bickering. Isn't that right, dear?"

Delaney frowned in response. She never liked mixing work with her home life.

"I thought the FBI wouldn't be concerned with such matters," Harper responded.

"Normally, we're not," Jones replied. "However, when your wife called me, she sounded distraught. I, therefore, agreed. Permit me to clarify, Seong-ho Moon, he's a friend of yours?"

"That's right. Is it illegal to have friends now?"

"Mr. Harper, I'm only trying to straighten things out. He flew to Havana at your behest, I believe. Having stayed a couple of days, he then flew back to the States. To Savannah, Georgia, to be precise, staying four nights at the Indigo Hotel. Then he returned to California. Sometime later, you wired $50,000 to Mr. Moon's bank account."

"It's a crime to help a guy in need of a vacation, I suppose?"

"Mr. Moon is not short of money in his own right. He has a high paying job and a healthy balance in his bank account. I checked. What was the money really for, Mr. Harper?"

"You tell me, Jonesy. You seem to have all the answers."

"No, I don't. Not yet, anyway. I tried contacting Mr. Moon. His employers tell me he's taken an extended leave of absence. Family emergency, I was told. Except, upon speaking with his parents, they know of no family crisis. In truth, they have no idea where their son is."

"Probably taking a world cruise. How's that for an emergency?" Harper suggested, flippantly.

"What do you know about funds being wired to a bank account in Cuba, for the benefit of a Federico Ramírez?"

"Federico is writing a biography of Fulgencio Batista. I gave him an advance."

"$50,000, to an unknown writer? Really."

"I'm a philanthropist. I like to encourage raw talent."

"Do you know how Mr. Ramírez spent the money, Harper?" Jones asked.

Trying to keep a poker face, Harper shook his head. Thus far, the Special Agent had not realized the Brazilian was sitting only yards away from them.

"Is that a no, or are you not saying?"

Achoo! Harper sneezed. "I think I'm starting a cold."

"If you're not going to talk to me, Harper, perhaps you'll speak to *Teniente* Guillén. He has a long list of questions for you."

Harper sighed, resigning himself to another bout of cross-examination.

"*Señor* Harper, you entered the country illegally," Guillén began. "There is no record of you passing through Immigration."

"Must be a clerical error. Not my fault if you cannot get your act together."

"Do you have your passport and visa on you?"

"Fortunately, I didn't bring it with me today. If I did, you'd be looking at soggy pieces of paper." Harper laughed.

The police officer ignored the misplaced humor and switched his line of questioning. "Tell me, *señor*, did you hire a fishing boat from the Marina recently, captained by José Enriques Ruiz?"

"What if I did?"

"The next day, the body of *Captán* Ruiz washed ashore. At the time, everyone assumed he had fallen overboard accidentally and drowned. Now I'm not so sure."

"You seriously think I killed the captain?" Harper scoffed. "No way are you pinning that on me."

"Then answer me this. Do you know Nicolás Marcolata, the former priest of the *Iglesia de Nuestra Señora de la Merced?* I say *former* because he was recently murdered. Your fingerprints, kindly provided by the FBI, were a match to those found at the scene."

"I knew Father Marcolata," Harper admitted. "He befriended me, let me stay at his home. But I didn't stab him."

"Did I mention how he was killed, *señor* Harper?" Guillén remarked.

Shit, thought Harper. *Me and my big mouth.*

"Then there are the questions of you using a drone without a permit, trying to recruit Russian immigrants for a private army you were forming, and lastly, procuring smoke grenades by bribing a police officer."

"That last accusation wasn't me. That was ..." Harper stopped himself.

"Yes, *señor* Harper; you were about to say?"

"... was no one I know." *Me and my big mouth, again.*

"I don't believe you, *señor*. Are you plotting a revolution?"

"HERE WE GO, AGAIN," HARPER REMARKED PITHILY. "YOU'VE seen this movie before, Jonesy. It's the one where the hero gets shafted." Turning to address Delaney and Guillén as well, he continued, "Do you guys seriously believe that I was organizing a Mardi Gras out there in the tunnel. Check your calendars. We're nowhere close to Fat Tuesday."

"What then, Mr. Harper?" Special Agent Delaney asked. "Can you account for the bunch of crazy locals running up and down the side tunnels shouting *El Coco?*"

The police officer scoffed, dismissively. "*El Coco* is a mythical ghost-monster. Parents tell their children, if they do not behave, *El Coco* will eat them or steal them away."

"Spare me the nursery rhyme," Harper interjected. "You're ignoring the big question. How many people have gone missing in the past month, Lieutenant Guillén? Is that the work of your mythical *El Coco?* Look around you, *señor,* and you will find a more plausible explanation. The victims now being hauled out of this tank were subjected to Daniels' experiments. Search the tunnels. I am sure you will find more."

"Experiments? For what purpose?" Jones asked.

"Not being a scientist, I defer to those more knowledgeable, but as a layman, I'd say their brains were being networked to form a human supercomputer. And what you're viewing today is only the tip of the iceberg. These experiments have been going on for decades. Sadly, for those abducted, with fatal results. I can even show you how they disposed of the bodies."

"You keep saying experiments, *señor* Harper. Who is conducting them?"

"A Doctor Daniels."

"A highly respected member of the community," *Teniente* Guillén remarked. "My *Capitán* plays golf with him once or twice a month."

"And do they discuss torturing and killing people? Probably not. Track down Daniels' notebooks. He's such an arrogant bastard he's probably recorded every sordid detail. And I'm sure, with a little friendly persuasion, Günter, here, will fill in the blanks."

The police Lieutenant turned to a sergeant and gave instructions to begin the search. "That still does not exonerate you from other charges you may be facing."

"Lord, give me strength." Harper turned his eyes to the ceiling. "Before you decide to throw me in jail, will somebody please find me some dry clothes?"

SEONG-HO HEARD THE SOUND OF MUSIC AND LAUGHTER AS HE ascended the second flight of stairs to Karmina's apartment. The door was open. As he entered, the Korean recognized a handful of neighbors. Apart from Harper and Federico, everyone else was a stranger.

"We wondered where you had got to," Harper remarked as soon as he pushed his way to the front of the crush. "Welcome to the party."

"What's the celebration?" Seong-ho asked.

"Daniels' demise, of course, but I forgot you haven't heard. He disappeared, along with Karmina, when the machinery he was using for his experiments activated."

"Let me get this straight. You're holding a party, and Karmina is missing?"

"A candlelight vigil as well. It could have been yours, too, if you hadn't shown up."

"Harper, I congratulate you on your lack of concern. I was nearly killed chasing after Mitchell."

"Is that where you went? I assumed you chickened out." The

Korean stared daggers at Harper. "Don't take things so seriously. I was only joking."

"It was no joke when Mitchell stole the motorcycle. I lost my phone and wallet, trying to climb out of a disused missile silo. Without money, I had to hitch a ride. And what's with that cryptic message you left at the priest's place?"

"That was Federico's idea, in case you went there first, instead of coming here."

"Leaving me to look up the verse in a Spanish bible, translate, and decode. Thanks a bunch. John 7:53: *And everyone went home.* It took me forever to realize it meant *return to the apartment.* Next time, leave a message in plain English," Seong-ho requested.

"And where's the fun in that?" Harper responded with a smirk. "Anyway, the prodigal son has returned safely."

"So what have you been doing while I've been away, apart from partying and missing me?" the Korean inquired.

"I've spoken to Julia on the phone; told her I was not dead. She seemed very pleased about that. I shall be able to leave Havana soon."

"And how did you swing that, Harper?"

"Along with the Cuban police, the FBI turned up at Daniels' underground bunker, . They informed me, Julia had contacted them after I wired funds to Federico's bank account. Never could work out how that broke the law, but the Bureau's presence sure helped cut through a lot of red tape. Of course, their boffins are ever so excited about the Doctor's research."

"About that. What was Daniels doing, exactly?"

"Developing a teleportation device," Harper replied matter-of-factly, offering the Korean a cold beer.

"Sounds like science fiction, if you ask me, Harper. Did it work?"

"Hard to say. So far, neither Daniels nor Karmina have turned up."

"Presumably, Daniels managed to escape," the Koran concluded.

"So, where is Karmina?" Harper asked.

"She'll show up, sooner or later."

"I hope you're right, Seong-ho. Poor Federico. He must be out of his mind with worry. We should go over and try to cheer him up."

The pair found Federico alone, leaning over the balcony.

"What are your plans, Federico? Are you still going to write that Batista biography?" the American asked.

"Not for the moment. I'm going to join the search for Karmina. I hear you're going back to the States, Harper."

"That's right. My wife has just informed me that I have a baby daughter. Her name is Ophelia."

"That's a beautiful name. What about you, Seong-ho? What are your plans?" the Brazilian inquired.

"I have to return to California. I expect my boss wants me back at work."

"Do you have a girl waiting for you there?" Federico asked, wistfully.

"I'm not sure Seong-ho has ever had a girlfriend," Harper interjected before the Korean could answer. "Oh no, I'm wrong. I am forgetting. Her name is *Ruby*; the computer programing language that is."

THE FOLLOWING MORNING, HARPER HAD TAKEN HIMSELF TO AN outdoor café and sat alone at a table, enjoying the solitude of his own company. A man approached and took the chair opposite, without waiting for an invitation.

"Kirt Mitchell, you snake in the grass, what are you doing here?"

"I was hoping we could put the past behind us, bro," Harper's former gambling partner replied. "Become friends again."

"Friends? We were never friends, Mitchell. You only befriended me to further your own ends. Go away and leave me alone."

Mitchell ignored the request.

"Leave now, before I do something I'll regret."

"Come on, Harper. You can't deny me a cold beer, surely. A quick drink together for old times sake." Mitchell caught the waiter's attention and placed his order.

A long five minutes of stony silence followed, during which time Harper distracted himself by watching the locals go about their business. "And why should I drink with you?" Harper eventually asked as the waiter returned to their table.

Mitchell picked up his glass. "Cheers, bro. Or should I say ¡salud!

What's the matter, Harper, not drinking with me? After all, I did save your life."

Harper scoffed but listened. Mitchell described how he had deflected Bernhart's aim when he fired a handgun during the confrontation in the underground facility.

"You're making it up. The Argentinian wasn't shooting at me. Besides, you weren't even there," the American asserted.

"I was in the next room, bro. With a little practice, it's amazing how far a mind probe can reach. But you know the technicalities already, don't you, Harper?"

"Mitchell, you talking a load of horse shit."

"Take a trip into my head, if you like. I'm telling the truth."

"Mmm; that's not conclusive," Harper told him after a quick mind-meld. "Midnight, I know you are faking those thoughts because Seong-ho tells a different story."

Mitchell took a long swig of beer. "If you say so, bro. Just trying to offer you an olive branch, that's all. Tell me, what's that official-looking piece of paper on the table. Are they going to give you a medal?"

"If you must know, the FBI has given me immunity from prosecution over the Phelps' killing."

Mitchell nearly choked on his drink as he burst out laughing. "Immunity from prosecution? They're yanking your chain, bro. Phelps is alive and kicking. His death was staged."

"But I …"

"But what, bro? You killed him; is that what you remember? What the eye sees is not necessarily what the brain records. You can understand that. They duped you, *amigo*. The closed-circuit camera's recording, that was bogus as well."

"And you know all this; how?"

"Because I saw Daniels talking to Phelps a week ago. I expect both of them are somewhere in South America by now. Setting up another little venture, no doubt." Mitchell laughed again. "Duped. Duped. You have been well and truly duped."

"All right, Midnight. Say I do believe you. Going back to my first question, apart from annoying me, what are you doing here?"

"I've come with a business proposition, bro. The original formula you found, not the altered one; you still have it?"

Harper did not reply.

"I'll take that as a yes. It's got to be worth a fortune to some pharmaceutical company. I have connections, you know."

"But, Midnight, it doesn't work."

"With a little tweaking, it will. We'd both be millionaires, ten times over."

"Have you any idea what that drug does, Mitchell?"

"Nope and neither do I care. Just show me the money, bro. Show me the money."

Harper took a deep breath. A quick probe into Kirt Mitchell's head and he confirmed the man was deadly serious. Then he replied, "No. Over my dead body, nobody is going to get their hands on that formula."

Mitchell shrugged off his look of disappointment. "Okay, bro; if that's what you want." After taking another sip of beer from his glass, he added, "Be careful what you wish for bro; that's all I can say."

"Mitchell, I can feel you. Stay out of my head. And stay out of my life. Understand that!"

"THAT WAS QUITE AN ARGUMENT BETWEEN YOU AND YOUR FRIEND," were the first words uttered by the smartly dressed lady that approached Harper's table.

"You heard," he replied, recognizing the speaker as Special Agent Margaret Delaney of the FBI.

"You were talking so loud, practically everyone did. May I sit down and join you?"

Harper begrudgingly nodded to a vacant chair, preferring his own company. "Any develops on the whereabouts of Doctor Daniels and Karmina?"

"I'm afraid not." Delaney paused when a waiter approached and took her order of a cup of coffee. When the man was out of earshot, she continued. "We have a team going over Daniels's equipment. They are hoping to get some clue as to what may have happened."

"They vanished into thin air. It's as simple as that," Harper reminded her.

"Making that one hell of a magic trick. I'm not buying it, Mr. Harper." Delaney smiled as if she were patiently enlightening a young child. "Daniels, I expect, used the darkness to escape. He has to be somewhere."

"That's what Seong-ho Moon thinks. Maybe Karmina followed him?"

"You could be right, Harper. Only time will tell."

Harper tensed his facial muscles in exasperation. "If that's the case, Karmina should have contacted Federico by now. I fear something bad has happened to her."

"Let's hope not. Remember the adage; no news is good news," Delaney counseled.

"If you say so." Unconvinced by his own words, Harper's brows drew together as he bit his lower lip.

"Cheer up. I have a present for you." The Special Agent slid an envelope across the table.

"What is this, a Father's Day card?"

"Stop being a cynic, Harper. Open it and see."

"An American passport." Looking inside, he added, "In my real name. Does this mean I am free to leave Cuba?"

Delaney smiled again. "And return to the United States. However, there is one condition."

"What is it his time?"

"You sign the piece of paper that still tucked inside the envelope."

Harper pulled it out. "A non-disclosure agreement. I knew there would be a catch."

"Your choice, Harper. You can stay here and play tourist, or you can go join your family."

"You know where they are?"

"We've been keeping an eye on Mrs. Montgomery's house ever since the shooting," Delaney replied matter-of-factly.

"Shooting? What shooting? Was anybody hurt?"

"A man named Conrad White was killed by your Aunt Cordelia, during a home invasion."

"No one else?"

"No. Apart from being shaken up, your family is fine.

Incidentally, if the description is correct, the man you were conversing with a few minutes ago accompanied White."

"Mitchell? That douchebag. I might have guessed. Aren't you going to arrest him?"

"Not my jurisdiction. May I remind you, we're in Cuba, Harper. Now sign the NDA, and we can both get out of here. I have a company jet waiting at the airport, heading back to DC. Savannah is hardly any detour at all. You're welcome to a lift. What do you say?"

"There is nothing *to* say except *can I borrow your pen*?"

WITHIN A FEW DAYS OF ARRIVING AT CORDELIA'S RESIDENCE, ROGER Harper had readjusted to the routine of family life. This evening he had been sweet-talked into playing the property trading game, *Monopoly*. Spencer went first. She threw a double one and moved her penguin token to *Community Chest*. Picking up a card, it read MISS A TURN.

Oliver was next. He counted eight squares. His Tyrannosaurus Rex token ended up on *Vermont Avenue*, which he purchased for $100.

Next up was Julia. Her dice rolled to a stop and showed a four and a six. She ended up in jail, much to the hoots of delight from the children.

Aunt Cordelia's cat token landed on the railway station. She decided to pass up the opportunity to purchase the deed.

Harper was the last to go. Before he threw the dice, he swapped out the top hat token for the 1952 Cuban silver coin that he carried around as a lucky charm. Oliver declared he wanted one as well. Spencer joined in the protest. "Is suppose you want one too, Jules?"

His wife smiled and nodded, not wishing to be left out.

"Okay. Hang on a minute. I need to fetch something from next door." Harper left his chair and went into the dining room. After lifting out a plastic bag from one of the sideboard drawers, he returned and tipped the contents out onto the coffee table. "There. Everybody can choose one," he told them as five similar coins skidded across the surface.

"They are all the same," Oliver protested. "How will we tell the difference?"

"Look on the backs, son. They have different dates."

The children quickly turned three of them over.

1915 • 1948 • 1916 • 1920 • 1949

"Where did these come from, Roger?" Julia inquired.

"Olly told me how the coin inset into the key had come out and rolled under the piano. Later, I took a look. When I couldn't see it, I assumed it had fallen between a gap in the floorboards. Sure enough, it was in the basement, together with those you're looking at."

"How come so many?" was Julia's next question.

"I don't know. I'm no scientist," her husband replied. "Converging parallel universes, maybe. Federico's the person to ask. He comes up with bizarre scientific theories."

"Is that so. Give me an example," Julia asked.

"Well, there was a time when he, Seong-ho, and I were going to revisit *Juraguá*, the site of Cuba's unfinished nuclear power plant. He suggested taking a couple of aspirin before we left as a precaution against radiation sickness."

Julia found it hard to suppress a snicker.

"That's Federico for you. There were times when one never knew if he was serious or joking."

"You miss him, don't you, Roger?" Julia asked sympathetically, touching his arm.

"I do," Harper agreed. "Without his help, I may have never escaped prison. Sadly, I never got the opportunity to thank him." There was a brief silence, and then he continued, "Are we playing *Monopoly*, or what? I believe it's my throw."

Showers prevailed for the next seven days, keeping the children inside for much of the time. Sitting on the parlor floor, they were currently playing tiddlywinks with the coins found in the basement. The front doorbell rang.

Harper heard the sound of running feet, a door opening, and an inaudible conversation. Then more running feet, which stopped at the entrance to the dining room. "Dad, there's a lady at the door," announced Oliver. "Shall I show her in?"

"Did she give a name?"

"No, but she says she knows you."

"Does she have a badge?"

"Yes, Dad. It's made of gold and has the words *Federal Bureau of Investigation* at the top and *Department of Justice* at the bottom."

"Then invite the Bureau lady in, Olly. And tell your mother she's here?"

Oliver scampered off, returning with the Special Agent a minute later.

"Agent Delaney, to what do I owe the honor? Is this a social call or strictly business?"

"Nice to see you again, Harper." Delaney held out a hand in

greeting. "Business, I'm sorry to say. I hope you and your family are well."

"We are, thank you, as long as you're not here to arrest me."

Delaney smiled. "Nothing like that. May I sit down?"

"Yes, of course. Take a seat. And here comes Jules."

Julia Harper entered the room, carrying Ophelia. Delaney stood up, admired the infant, and started making cooing noises, which progressed into a rapid verbal exchange between the women as to how the baby was doing.

After a minute, Harper interrupted by coughing loudly.

"Sorry, Roger. I'll leave you and Ms. Delaney to talk. I'll go into the kitchen and make some lemonade. Olly, come with me. You can help."

Left alone with Harper, the Special Agent again sat down, but not before retrieving a manila folder from her oversized shoulder bag. Opening the file, she removed three photographs. Handing the first to Harper, she asked. "Anyone you recognize."

"Yuck," was the reaction. "You might have warned me."

"Oops. My bad. The bloating you are seeing, and the grayish wax-like film that has formed over the corpse, occurred during prolonged immersion in seawater. Nevertheless, does the photo jog your memory?" Harper stayed silent. "How about his one?"

The second picture was a close-up of the face.

"That is so gross. With the eyes and lips missing, it's difficult to say."

"I'm afraid that's a result of small fish feeding on the softer parts. What if I told you the victim was five feet four inches tall and weighed approximately one hundred twenty pounds?"

Harper looked at Delaney. Her eyes looked intently back, for any sign of recognition.

"Oh, my God. Is that Karmina, or what's left of her?"

"We believe it is. You are looking at one of two bodies washed up on Carova Beach, North Carolina."

"And the other?" Harper asked hesitantly. He was glad that Julia and Oliver were no longer in the room.

Delaney handed over another facial photograph and an X-ray

of a jaw. "We had more to go on with this one. Dental records confirm this to be none other than your old adversary, Daniels."

"So you're saying that after Karmina and the mad doctor vanish in Cuba, they end up on the North Carolina shoreline. That is incredible."

"It surely is," Delaney responded, after putting the photographs and X-ray back into the folder. "But that was not their initial destination. Our technical team has finally managed to decipher the setting on Daniel's machine, which turned out to be the coordinates 32°37'49.1"N 76°56'50.5"W. Smack in the Atlantic Ocean, 150 miles for the nearest landfall and 270 miles south-southwest of Carova Beach itself. We consulted with the Coast Guard, and they used some software called *SAROPS*, which stands for *Search and Rescue Optimal Planning System*. Given a known starting position, it attempts to predict where a body might end up relative to the nearby ocean currents. The start and finish points match up pretty well with their computer model."

"I recall Federico trying to stop the countdown. He must have moved the dials. I am sure Daniels did not intend to end up in the middle of the ocean. Poor Karmina, she gave her life to save me." Harper let out a deep sigh. "Has Federico been told?"

"The short version, yes," Delaney replied. "We spared him the gory details."

Julia walked in, carrying a tray of cold drinks. "Why the long faces? What's wrong?" she asked.

"I was just telling your husband we found Karmina's body," Margaret Delaney answered.

"Oh. I am sorry to hear that." Julia set the tray down on the dining table. "Help yourself to refreshments, Ms. Delaney. Where was it recovered?"

"A beach in North Carolina. However, the pertinent question is not *where*, but *when*?"

"I CANNOT BELIEVE SPECIAL AGENT DELANEY SAID THOSE photographs and reports dated back to 2006," Julia remarked to Harper as she readied herself for bed. "You're telling me that not only did that machine succeed in transporting them nearly eight hundred miles away from Havana, but it sent them back into the past. I thought time travel was impossible."

"You're in good company. Stephen Hawking did as well," her husband responded. "It's a shame he is no longer alive to be told otherwise. If he were, I bet he would have written a follow-up scientific paper."

Julia joined Harper in bed. "Are you going to read, or shall I turn out the light?"

"I'm going to sleep. I've had enough excitement for one day."

"Be sure you do. Don't lie there, mulling over things you can't change." She gave him a quick peck on the cheek and snuggled under the covers.

"We are all safe now; you, the children, and me," Harper told her as he spooned in behind her. "Hyde dies in the clock tower of the Houses of Parliament, London. Daniels ends up in a watery grave. And thanks to your Aunt Cordelia's quick thinking, that rogue Conrad White is pushing up daisies. Anyway, that quite enough of the bad guys. I love you, Jules. Sleep tight."

"I love you too, Roger Harper."

They settled in, and all was quiet until Julia suddenly jerked the covers.

"What is it, honeybee?" Harper asked.

"You're forgetting Midnight."

"Let's not worry about that black sheep. I don't believe the man has the *cojones* to do anything to threaten our family on his own."

"Roger; language."

"That's what they would say in Cuba," Harper replied.

"Don't let me catch you teaching Olly that, or you'll be in deep trouble."

Harper kissed his wife on the back of the neck in acknowledgment. "Kirt Mitchell is probably in a bar someplace hatching his next plot to cheat another poor sucker out of their winnings. Now, please, can we get some sleep?"

"I hope you're right, that's all."

Within minutes Harper was sound asleep.

Julia prayed silently to herself, *Dear Lord, let us have a quiet life for the next one hundred years.*

Five minutes passed. She was still awake.

And please, Lord, do something about Roger's snoring.

EIGHT MONTHS LATER, DURING THE CELEBRATION OF OLIVER'S birthday, the lad was opening a present from his parents.

"Wow!" Oliver claimed after unboxing a *Holy Stone Quadcopter Drone* complete with a high-definition camera. "What made you think of buying me this?"

"The drone is similar to the one used by Seong-ho when we were in Cuba," his father explained. "Pretty cool, huh?"

"Sure is," the boy replied.

Oliver began inserting one of the batteries.

"Don't think for one minute you're going to fly that thing in the house, young man," Julia admonished. "It's strictly an outdoor toy, Olly."

"It's not a toy," Harper interjected, "but your mother is right. To be used strictly outside."

"We can take it on adventures, Olly," Spencer suggested, "and I've bought you something to go with it."

Oliver began tearing off the wrapping.

After a brief inspection, he remarked. "It's a packet of spare parts. What do I need these for?"

"When you crash it, of course." The girl began to chuckle.

"Who says I'll crash?" Oliver asked indignantly.

"Me."

Julia cut in, before an argument ensued, "Oliver, say thank you to Spencer."

"Thank you," he replied. "Is it time to cut the cake? I'm hungry."

Cordelia excused herself, went to the kitchen, and returned with the birthday cake, which she set down on a nearby table. Under her arm was a large padded envelope.

"Another present for me?" the boy enthusiastically asked.

"Not this time. Oliver," his great aunt replied. "It came in the mail this morning, address to your mother. I was so busy preparing for your birthday party, I completely forgot all about it."

After briefly reading the return address, Julia began opening the packet.

Intrigued, for his mother rarely got mail, Oliver asked, "Who is it from, Mom?"

"From an attorney in Vancouver, if you must know," Julia replied.

Slowly she leafed through the contents, setting aside a legal document on the coffee table, together with some photographs, and a map highlighting a section of land beside a lake.

While the children viewed the snapshots showing a forested area abutting a lakeshore, Harper was trying to read the upside-down wording on the document.

Ignoring her husband's head-twisting antics, Julia concentrated on the cover letter.

"Well, I never," she uttered. "Who'd have thought."

"Thought what? Come on, Jules, spill the beans."

"Patience, Roger. You're worse than the kids. Why don't you all get yourselves some cake, and let me finish reading this? Then I will explain."

Attwell, Davis & Shaw LLP were estate attorneys with offices in Ottawa, Montreal, and Vancouver. Ellis Davis, the senior partner heading up the Vancouver operation, was the one who had been in touch with Julia a week earlier, informing her that her father had recently died, bequeathing her property in a remote region of British Columbia. The paperwork would follow, he told her, and that is what she had received today.

The surprise kicker in the cover letter was the property had been left in joint ownership with her half-sister. Until today she never knew her father had other daughter. However, later that evening, Cordelia confided that he had a reputation of being a rolling stone, seeking excitement, and starting new madcap enterprises. Without regard for his family, this impulse behavior was the reason her mother had insisted on a divorce.

Unaware of a failed marital relationships, as soon as the children found out Julia owned land in Canada, they wanted to visit.

"Please, Mom, say we can go," Oliver begged. "There's loads of time before the start of the autumn term. Dad can take me fishing."

"Maybe Spencer would like to do something else, for the remainder of the summer vacation," Julia suggested.

"There's a lake, and I like kayaking," her niece volunteered. "Swimming as well."

"Then we should go," Oliver declared.

"Not so fast, son," his father cautioned. "What's your mother going to be doing?"

"She can stay here and look after Ophelia."

"Remember the property has been left to *me*, Olly. I need to be there, and our sister comes with us. "

"Which means I'll get some quiet for a change," Cordelia told them.

There was a moment of silence as Oliver and Spencer looked at each other. Then they both grinned.

"Are you thinking what I'm thinking?" Spencer asked.

"I sure am," Oliver replied. Then, turning to face the older woman, he continued, "It's hardly fair you should be left by yourself. Why don't you come with us, Great-Aunt Cordelia?"

"At my age? That is a definite *no*," Cordelia responded. "As I said, I could do with a little quiet for a while."

"So be it," Harper agreed. "We shall miss you terribly, though."

"Tomorrow we can start packing. Who knows what we might find there? Buried treasure, sailing ships, and pirates, maybe? We might even meet Jack Sparrow."

Julia laughed. "Roger, stop teasing. There are no longer pirates in Canada."

"Oh, I hoped there would be." Oliver sounded downcast.

"Perhaps we'll come across Bigfoot," Spencer suggested. "Wouldn't that be exciting?"

"If you bring your camera, Spencer, you'll be able to take its photograph," Oliver proposed, eager to start their adventure.

"Canadians call it Sasquatch," Cordelia corrected. "Is the dog staying with me?"

"Certainly not," Spencer protested. "He's part of the family. Aren't you, boy?"

Shadow wagged his tail, enthusiastically, in agreement.

"In that case, we should not rely on commercial flights. I'll add chartering a plane to my checklist," Harper told them.

As Harper was stacking suitcases on the front porch, in readiness for their trip, a taxi pulled up in the driveway.

"Well, I never," he declared. "What brings you to this part of the world, Federico?" The American shook hands with the Brazilian and asked how he was feeling.

Choosing to ignore the question, Federico replied, "I've come to wish Oliver a happy birthday. It is today, isn't it?"

Harper smiled. "Three days ago actually, but not to worry. I think there is still some birthday cake left. Come inside and meet everyone."

Introductions over, the Brazilian reached into his satchel and produced a small box, gift wrapped in bright red paper. "Here, Oliver; I brought a present for you. Sorry, I'm a few days late."

Within seconds the boy had the box open. "Awesome. Thank you very much. Just what is needed when Spencer and I visit British Columbia."

"The compass will go with your telescope," Spencer told him. "That's made of brass too. We can use them when we go exploring together."

"You have relatives in British Columbia?" the Brazilian inquired.

"A half-sister," Julia replied. "My late father left us some property at the northern end of Little Harrison Lake. We're about to set off and check it out."

"Would you like to come with us?" Oliver asked. "And make sure Dad stays out of trouble."

Everyone laughed, except Harper.

"I expect Federico has other plans, Olly," his mother cautioned.

"I don't actually," the Brazilian countered. "I needed to get away from Cuba, that is all. The place holds painful memories since Karmina's death was confirmed."

"We heard. I'm so sorry, Federico," Julia said, placing a hand on his arm. "If there's anything we can do, please don't hesitate to ask."

"Thank you. You're very kind."

"What about your research on President Batista?" Harper asked.

"I have decided to abandon writing his biography. I'm thinking of a novel instead."

Oliver piped up, "Pirates would make a good story, with buried treasure and captured sailors forced to walk the plank."

"Or Sasquatch," Spencer chimed in. "There are rumors it lives near where we are going."

"Yes. Why don't you come with us?" Harper urged. "You'll have a few weeks of relaxation by a lake. We won't take no for an answer, will we, Jules?"

"Stop it, Roger. You're as bad as Olly and Spencer. Federico should be allowed to decide for himself."

"Dad has chartered a private jet," Oliver announced proudly. "There's plenty of room?"

"And there's a spare seat in the shuttle taking us to the airport," Harper added. "On the way, you can tell me all about this novel you're planning."

As the airplane headed northwest, cruising at thirty thousand feet, the older children took in the scenery. Over the intercom, the pilot was giving a running commentary.

"Below, and to our right, is the Flathead Indian Reservation," he told them. "Since 1855, it has been home to the *Bitterroot Salish, Kootenai*, and *Pend d'Oreilles* tribes. Based on archaeological findings, Native Americans have lived in Montana for more than fourteen thousand years."

"Did they hunt dinosaurs back then?" the boy asked.

"That's a stupid question, Olly," Spencer chided. "Dinosaurs died out sixty-six million years ago."

"Says who?"

"Says me," the girl countered.

"I don't believe you."

"Ask your mom. She'll tell you I'm right."

Julia decided not to get involved in the disagreement. Instead, she gazed out of the window, recalling the previous evening's telephone conversation when she introduced herself to Dalia, her half-sister. Ellis Davis had enclosed contact details in his letter. Dee, as she called herself, was as surprised as Julia to find she had a sibling.

With only name, address, and telephone number, Julia had little success searching the Internet. She did find, in the Faculty Directory of the University of British Columbia, Dalia listed as an Associate Professor Emeritus in the Anthropology Department, along with an email address. Nothing about her personal life, however.

Was making face-to-face contact a wise thing to do? Julia wondered. The nagging question hovered at the back of her mind, keeping her on edge.

On the other hand, Harper was totally relaxed. His seat in the reclined position, eyes closed, he was contemplating a few weeks of peaceful relaxation. However, as Roger Harper would soon find out, enjoying a quiet life is an extremely elusive commodity.

THE END

PLEASE POST A REVIEW

We hope you enjoyed reading *The Man Who Could Not Cheat Time*. Please post a review at the source of purchase and on GoodReads. You will be helping others decide whether or not to read the book, and hopefully make us better authors in the future.

Thank you.

JGR & BR

www.ingramcontent.com/pod-product-compliance
Lightning Source LLC
Chambersburg PA
CBHW020315200626
46814CB00006BA/2247